Having previously worked as a journalist and then a psychotherapist, Caroline Dunford enjoyed many years helping other people shape their personal life stories before taking the plunge and writing her own novels. She has now published almost thirty books in genres ranging from historical crime to thrillers and romance. Caroline also teaches creative writing courses part-time at the University of Edinburgh.

For further information about Caroline Dunford's Euphemia Martins mysteries, and to find out all about Caroline's Second World War series, featuring Euphemia's perceptive daughter Hope Stapleford, visit: caroline-dunford.squarespace.com.

Praise for Caroline Dunford's novels:

'A sparkling and witty crime debut with a female protagonist to challenge Miss Marple' Lin Anderson

'Impeccable historical detail with a light touch' Lesley Cookman

'Euphemia Martins is feisty, funny and completely adorable' Colette McCormick

'A rattlingly good dose of Edwardian country house intrigue with plenty of twists and turns and clues to puzzle through' *Booklore.co.uk*

'The sharp dialogue capture(s) the feel of the era . . . an engaging and entertaining read' *Portobello Book Blog*

By Caroline Dunford

Euphemia Martins Mysteries:

A Death in the Family
A Death in the Highlands
A Death in the Asylum
A Death in the Wedding Party
The Mistletoe Mystery (a short story)
A Death in the Pavilion
A Death in the Loch
A Death for King and Country
A Death for a Cause
A Death by Arson
A Death Overseas
A Death at Crystal Palace
A Death at a Gentleman's Club
A Death at the Church
A Death at the Races
A Death in the Hospital
A Death on Stage
A Death of a Dead Man
A Death at Christmas

Hope Stapleford Series:

Hope for the Innocent
Hope to Survive
Hope for Tomorrow
Hope Under Fire

Others:

Highland Inheritance
Playing for Love
Burke's Last Witness

A DEATH AT CHRISTMAS

CAROLINE DUNFORD

Copyright © 2025 Caroline Dunford

The right of Caroline Dunford to be identified as the Author of
the Work has been asserted by her in accordance with the Copyright,
Designs and Patents Act 1988.

First published in 2025 by Headline Accent
An imprint of Headline Publishing Group Limited

1

Apart from any use permitted under UK copyright law, this publication may
only be reproduced, stored, or transmitted, in any form, or by any means,
with prior permission in writing of the publishers or, in the case of
reprographic production, in accordance with the terms of licences
issued by the Copyright Licensing Agency.

All characters in this publication are fictitious and any resemblance
to real persons, living or dead, is purely coincidental.

Cataloguing in Publication Data is available from the British Library

Paperback ISBN 978 1 4722 9539 2

Typeset in 10.5/13pt Bembo Std by Six Red Marbles UK, Thetford, Norfolk

Printed and bound in Great Britain by Clays Ltd, Elcograf S.p.A.

Headline's policy is to use papers that are natural, renewable and recyclable
products and made from wood grown in well-managed forests and other
controlled sources. The logging and manufacturing processes are expected
to conform to the environmental regulations of the country of origin.

Headline Publishing Group Limited
An Hachette UK Company
Carmelite House
50 Victoria Embankment
London EC4Y 0DZ

The authorised representative in the EEA is Hachette Ireland,
8 Castlecourt Centre, Dublin 15, D15 XTP3, Ireland (email: info@hbgi.ie)

www.headline.co.uk
www.hachette.co.uk

For Graham and the boys.
Also my writing group – Tim, Andrew and Alba.
With thanks to my hard-working agent Amy Collins of
Talcott Notch, and, of course, my publisher.

Dramatis Personae

Euphemia Stapleford – wife of Bertram Stapleford and spy. Code name 'Alice'

Bertram Stapleford – husband of Euphemia, ex-SIS operative, put-upon

Fitzroy – dashing British spy and Euphemia's partner in espionage

Hans Muller – brother-in-law to Bertram, married to Richenda, handsome and knows it

Esmeralda – young widow met and wooed by Hans during *A Death of a Dead Man*

Winifred Mansfield – an older lady who is very keen on knitting

The Grubers – a loud red-faced man and his much younger and gentler blond wife

Baron von Nacht (Alex) – a poser, very sharp and old compatriot of Fitzroy

The Smiths and their three sons – a quiet couple with large, indistinguishable 'sons'

Mimi and Gertrude – two spinster sisters

Charles 'Charlie' Bingham – coarse Londoner with little imagination

Col. Mathew Long – English colonel with imposing beard

Lt Jerry Wools – his adjutant, has an eye for the ladies

Ruby Milton – extremely glamorous young woman of foreign origin

Lucinda Scarlatti – another extremely glamorous young woman of foreign origin

Richenda – Hans's wife, and an unexpected guest
Richenda's maid – discreet and barely noticed
Rory McLeod – Special Branch policeman who has a long and complicated history with Euphemia
Lady Jane – Rory's adoring wife
John Groats – an overbearing American
Barnabas Willoughby – clumsy footman and junior spy
Jack – a bull terrier, who owns Fitzroy
Griffin – Fitzroy's major-domo, torrid past history
Diverse servants and neighbours of no real significance

Chapter One

Fitzroy Announces His Christmas Extravaganza

'So do you have a theme for our Christmas extravaganza yet?' asked Fitzroy.

It is rare for the spymaster to deprive me of words. I have known him a long time. Long enough to even know his Christian name is Eric, although I remain unsure about his surname. He promised me, near the start of our relationship as co-workers, that he would never lie to me. And he doesn't. He does, however, frequently commit the sin of omission.

'What Christmas extravaganza?' I asked, injecting as much ice as possible into my tone.

Fitzroy brushed this off, as easily as water off the proverbial duck's back. 'Oh, your husband knows all about it. He's totally on board.'

'Bertram knows?'

'Unless you have divorced and remarried without my knowledge, which is highly unlikely for multiple reasons I shall not enumerate. Yes, Bertram knows all about it.'

'Will you kindly stop speaking nonsense and tell me what is going on?'

Fitzroy stretched his long legs out in front of the fire and positively lazed in his chair. A thing no gentleman should do in the presence of a lady, but he is, as he would remind me often, no gentleman. This, despite being the son of a duke – if that part can be believed. He has, after all, never told me which duke or even made the slightest attempt to introduce me to his family. This, despite the fact he often makes himself at home in *my* family.

We were sitting in the smaller saloon in White Orchards, an estate Bertram had bought without consulting me, and which was in all manner of ways quite awful. Bertram loves the wildness of the Fens, and the bleak flat open landscapes. I do not. I much prefer being in town, or really anywhere else. Fitzroy also seems to enjoy the environs and as he so often stops by between missions we have given him his own set of rooms, which he rather rudely locks up when he is not present. I have yet to tell Bertram that he not only locks the rooms, but has in fact changed the lock.

Before the war we worked together, but more and more he is going on solo missions that I suspect take him behind enemy lines. Our boss, Morley, who in most cases Fitzroy never heeds much, has taken to heart the idea that being of the female persuasion I must not go into hostile territory. It is quite ridiculous. I have often been in hostile lands, and faced hostile foes; why the outbreak of actual war should make this any different I have no idea. For now, more than ever, they need good field agents. As Fitzroy says, and this is true, espionage has two purposes. Ideally it prevents the outbreak of open warfare. When this fails, it is used to bring the conflict to a speedier end than the Top Brass (as Fitzroy calls them in a voice dripping with sarcasm) can manage.

'Why am I hosting a house party? I hope you're not expecting people to dance.'

'Don't you have a ballroom?' said Fitzroy, frowning.

'Good God, man, you're here often enough to know the estate inside out.'

He blinked a bit at that. 'I suppose I didn't really think about it. I just assumed . . .'

'That I had a ballroom lying around here somewhere in this nasty little—' I broke off as my husband strolled into the saloon, a newspaper tucked under his arm. He bent down and gave me a peck on the cheek.

'I was wondering if you might like a game of chess before luncheon, my dear?'

'We are in the middle of a serious conversation,' said Fitzroy with some impatience.

'Talking about a nasty little what?' said Bertram, standing up and raising an eyebrow at the spy. I gave Fitzroy a rather imploring look, and I saw the corners of his mouth twitch. He had me, as he might say rather crudely, over a barrel.

'Your wife was referring to the edge of your south lawn. It has been afflicted with some virulent infestation, and she was concerned that it might look unfortunate during the house party.'

'Infestation,' said Bertram in a worried voice, as he flopped into a chair. His newspaper fell to the ground unheeded. He is something of a germophobe. Although, to be fair, he has a weaker constitution than most.

'Little green flies or some such thing. Your gardener will be able to sort it out. Euphemia isn't, at heart, a country girl. It's nothing at all to worry about. Now what theme do you think we should have for the house party?'

'Well, I've been thinking about that,' said my husband, bestowing a condescending smile on me, and settling back against the cushions. 'Did you say there was a budget, Fitzroy?'

'A budget, not a windfall!'

'Oh tosh, we'll use our own people. Will hardly cost a penny. They're damn good at doing such things – the ones who haven't already gone to war, that is.'

Fitzroy gave me a look that clearly said, 'They would need to be.' I didn't find it funny, and turned my gaze on the Persian carpet. It would need to be cleaned properly before we had proper visitors.

'Anyway, I was thinking,' continued Bertram, 'that we could modify the doors between here and the drawing room, and turn it into a ballroom in case we want to dance. The other saloon and the morning room would suffice for the buffet and a resting area. Then people could spill over into the hallway.'

'How many people are coming?' I asked in horror.

'Between thirty and fifty, I should think,' said Fitzroy. 'Plus your own family.'

'We cannot house so many people!' I said in horror.

'Yes, well,' said Fitzroy, 'you'd be amazed where bachelors will sleep. One can always fit in more people than one imagines. All works out. Especially at Christmas. All good cheer and all that.'

'We can't,' I protested.

'Afraid you'll have to,' said Fitzroy. 'Some of the invitations have already gone out.'

'But we haven't even decided a date!'

'The thirteenth of December, with a couple of days either side for those travelling, and some general discussion. You should be free of them for Christmas itself. Just myself and whoever else of the family you choose to invite. Same as usual. It's about time you did a Christmas dinner for the neighbours too, isn't it? If you really don't have enough room, you could cajole them into helping out with a special dinner later.' He rose and smoothed out his jacket. 'It'll be fun. You'll enjoy it, Euphemia. Must be ages since you and Bertram had a good dance.'

'It's another bloody diplomatic attempt to end the war, isn't it? Last time we tried that, things went from bad to worse.'

'Well, the body was a little inconvenient, I admit. However, this time there won't be a politician in sight.'

'Then who?'

'Who else but people like us? Spies, Euphemia, spies!'

Chapter Two

Bertram Overheats

It was the most ridiculous and ill-considered scheme I had ever heard of – a spy party. What arrant nonsense.

Fitzroy, having announced the plan, promptly disappeared the next day, leaving me torn between worry that he had gone back behind enemy lines and annoyance that he was simply hiding from my ire. If the army had formally commandeered our home, I should not have been happy, but at least it would have been a straightforward matter. But this! Another crazy idea of my spying partner. It might be genius, but it was equally likely – or more likely – to be an utter disaster.

The consequences of this plot didn't bear thinking about. How our boss, Morley, had been talked into this, I had no idea. But whether I wanted the thing or not, by the time the scheme was revealed to me, Fitzroy and Bertram between them had it well under way. Mrs T, my capable housekeeper, was already sorting out the accommodations. Our cook, Mrs Warburton, moaning loudly about so much work, had already stocked up on provisions, pickled everything imaginable, had the ice house checked, made pie after pie, and was now testing various recipes out on us with varying degrees of success. In other words, she was enjoyed herself enormously. Our butler, Giles, strode about doing some serious butlering preparation. This, I suspected, included sorting and rearranging not only our wine cellar, but the large crates of wines and spirits that had started to arrive at the house. Always immaculate, a sole strand of hair now bounced on his forehead as he made his way busily about the house. If he went on like this for much longer he would need a new jacket, his chest was becoming so puffed up with pride.

It was all as unstoppable as a steam train. My only recourse was an attempt to modify the damage. And even there I was thwarted. Griffin, Fitzroy's major-domo, had arrived and was conferring with my housekeeper, Mrs T. Instead of being appalled by this excess during wartime, she, like my cook, had thrown herself wholeheartedly into the scheme and was suggesting even more things that could be pickled, poached and candied. Along with Giles, they spent evenings, from what Griffin told me, poring over dinner menus and seating arrangements. The latter was proving especially hard to do as they did not know who was attending. Instead, they spent time imagining possible guests and arranging them. Griffin told me it had become quite the evening parlour game below stairs.

We were still some weeks from the event when I entered the hall and smelt the distinctive aroma of Christmas cakes baking. Cinnamon, cloves and something subtly citrus. It was quite divine, and if I hadn't known for whom they were being cooked I would have been quite cheered. As it was, I went to hunt down Bertram in the smoking room and give him a piece of my mind.

Obviously, a smoking room is for the gentlemen alone. It is an utterly disgusting habit, but Bertram had installed his room before he married me, and it was one of his few pleasures now that he had become too unwell to ride. Although it was barely past midday I found him ensconced behind a left-wing newspaper that he occasionally writes for, pipe in his mouth, puffing like a small dragon, and with a brandy at his elbow. I moved stealthily towards him.

'I don't know why you should consider yourself safe in here,' I said. 'I have been known on more than one occasion to—'

I got no further as Bertram started in surprise at being so accosted. The newspaper fell from his hands, and the pipe from his slackened jaw. His brandy, caught by the edge of his rising elbow, went wild and hurtled across the room spraying alcohol left and right. I managed to dart back so it missed me. 'Dear God, woman, do you want to give me a heart attack?'

Obviously, I wanted to do nothing of the kind, but I said, 'If that gave you a shock wait until you have a house filled with spies! You have no idea what they will get up to. There will be shocks around every corner.'

'Dammit, Euphemia! I used to be involved in the spy-game too. Don't you think I know what's involved?'

I cast my eyes down and said, 'Your paper is on fire.'

Bertram stood up and immediately trod on the offending article, but he had forgotten he was wearing soft slippers, which began to smoulder. I gave a cursory look around the room and located the soda fountain. I snatched this up and spurted soda water copiously over Bertram's feet. 'Are you hurt?' I asked.

'Those were my favourite tartan slippers, Euphemia. I had only just worn them in.' He sat down again and began to examine the ruins.

These were not the most auspicious circumstances in which I could persuade my husband to cancel the party and repel all boarders (in the form of Fitzroy).

This was of course exactly what I wanted. Since Bertram's health had forced him to take a back seat, I had gone on missions with Fitzroy where I had been shot at, was frequently in terrible peril and had even been forced on some occasions to take a life. I had been circumspect describing my adventures when I returned home, as I did not wish to cause Bertram extra worry. As I am a fully fledged agent of the Crown, he didn't have the option of demanding his lady wife stay home. But now as I watched him picking mournfully at his slippers I knew I did not want to tell him the truth of what I experienced – ever. He had an image of me that not only he cherished, but I realised then and there I also cherished.

'I do not want to bring the business into our home.'

Bertram looked up and frowned. 'You have a secret office here. That man has his own rooms that he locks – locks in my own house. And we have had political parties before.'

'Firstly, Fitzroy may lock the doors all he likes, but both Mrs T and I have master keys,' I lied. Bertram opened his mouth to protest, but I caught the complaint before it was uttered. 'You had one too, but you have misplaced it. And, yes, we had a party with diplomats and politicians. This is a far different event. These are spies, dammit! They might all be foreign Fitzroys!'

Bertram paled at the thought but shook his head like a hunting dog shaking off the miseries of lake water. 'Don't swear, Euphemia. It doesn't suit you. Aping that damned man,' growled my husband.

'Look, Fitzroy is being opaque about this whole thing. He seems to think he has everyone under control, and yet he doesn't even know who is coming.'

'Of course he does,' blustered Bertram. 'Well, he knows who he has invited. There's a war on, dontcha know! Not all of them might be able to get across.'

'No, they might be preoccupied acting against the Empire!'

He coughed in an angry way that he knew I particularly disliked. 'That man assured me that invitees are professionals, and no side events, such as an ad hoc assassination, will occur. He has their word.'

'Fitzroy keeps his word on the rare occasions he chooses to give it,' I said more gently. 'But there is no reason to think another spy would do the same.'

'Like yourself, you mean?'

I was so utterly insulted by this remark that I walked out of the room.

'Ring the bell for the maid,' Bertram called after me. I gave the bell-pull a short, firm grasp and the wretched thing came away in my hand. I left it on the ground and stalked off.

Which is how Bertram and I became on non-speaking terms for the longest time in our relationship. In all, apart from the occasional 'please pass the salt', I don't think we spoke for the better part of two weeks. Perhaps, if I had been more patient and tried gently to explain the risks, he would have seen sense and closed the event down. As it was, I was angry at having my word called into question, and also contrarily so, because Bertram was completely right.

I would not hesitate to break my word if I deemed it necessary. The whole male code of honour has always seemed of a childish nature to me. I believe in doing what is necessary and getting the thing done. I already knew that both Fitzroy and Bertram would be appalled if I explained my perspective. So instead of helping in any way with the preparations, I retreated to my office and continued with the logistical planning I had been assigned while Fitzroy was in the field. I was so short-tempered with everyone that the household began to avoid me. Thus, I became both offended and rather lonely, which only embittered me further. I shunned the marital bed, and Bertram did not come looking for me. I suspect he was scared.

Chapter Three

I Realise What Has to be Done

'Peace offering?'

A ginger-haired man with a short moustache popped his head around my office door. He held out an enormous bouquet of red roses that clashed quite hideously with his colouring.

'You've stopped dyeing your hair,' I said. I stayed seated. Fitzroy came into the room and shut the door behind him.

'You're lucky I had time to bathe and shave. Been in the field for three weeks – and I do mean the ruddy field. Apart from deploring the death, blood and general slaughter, I do so hate the mud that comes with warfare.'

I looked at him more closely. The skin on his face had paled to an unhealthy grey, and while it stretched taut over the lower half of his face, and was hollowed by his cheekbones, there were new lines around his eyes. I got up and took the roses. 'You've had a bad time. Your face is full of shadows.'

Fitzroy sat down on my desk, dislodging and then ignoring the papers he knocked on to the floor. 'Do you know, I don't think I have ever bought you flowers before, have I?' he said in a bright voice.

'I shouldn't imagine you have bought them for Morley either.'

'Oh dear, do you think he will be jealous? Perhaps I shouldn't put that in my report?' He hit his hand on his forehead. 'What was I thinking? If Dotty learns of this, I'll never hear the last of it. I should send her some pansies. I think she's more of an herbaceous border type, don't you?'

'I haven't the slightest idea what an herbaceous border is, but I understand you are not going to fill me in on what you have been doing.'

'I might,' he said, dropping his playful tone, 'but only when I can face it myself again. The Christmas party, Alice, it has to work. The way things are over there – it's unspeakable – hell on earth – and a waste of life.' He got up abruptly and turned his back to me. I waited for him to get himself back under control. On a mission, Fitzroy was cold, focused and dispassionate. I was one of the few people he ever let see how what he had to do affected him. Fortunately, there came a loud scratching at the door.

I got up and opened it at once, and Jack, Fitzroy's English bull terrier, ran into the room. He jumped up at his master and whiffled enthusiastically in that odd way bull terriers do.

Fitzroy knelt down, still keeping his face turned from mine, and pulled the little dog's ears affectionately. 'Yes, I'm back now, boy. I'm here all Christmas and New Year.'

A tart response of *Really? How nice of you to inform us!* rose to my lips, but I kept it behind my teeth. Taking potshots at Fitzroy when he was like this was not sporting. I put the flowers on my desk and knelt down to pat the little dog too. He became extremely affectionate and made a good job of washing my face. 'Ugh,' I scolded, 'now I will have to wash again.' But I kissed him on his nose.

'So the pup succeeds where roses and others have failed,' said Fitzroy, finally looking at me again. 'I've been told you turned into quite the termagant while I was away.' The twinkle was back in his eye.

'Pah!' I said, standing up. 'You are the root of all the trouble here.'

'I like to think I leave a mark. Go and wash your face and get your coat. I think it's time we went for a walk together.' His expression became more serious. 'There are things I need to tell you.'

The air was sharply cold against my cheek, and the gathering dusk heralded an icy night. I could smell the dark, smoky, consoling aroma of a bonfire in the distance. Jack ran ahead of us, his paws breaking through the thin ice on little puddles and making a crack-crack sound that he seemed to enjoy. Every now and then he turned on the spot trying to repeat the noise and giving a small whiffle.

'Good walking shoes?' asked Fitzroy.

I nodded.

'Wrapped up warm?'

'You're not going to whisk me away somewhere, are you?'

'No, I'm a bit too fatigued for any whisking.' He flashed me a smile that shone white in the gloom, reminding me of the Cheshire Cat from *Alice in Wonderland*. 'No, I want to have a conversation alone with you, and I fear it may take some time.'

'That sounds serious,' I said. 'Is it a new briefing?'

'No, I'm going to tell you some of what I have seen. I apologise now for what I will say, but you need to understand my reasoning. I need you on board, Alice. Without you, I can't make this work.' Once again he had used my code name instead of my given name. Always a sign he was being serious.

'I doubt that. You are extremely competent.'

'Highly professional and obnoxiously talented, one might say. I still can't do this without you.' He stopped walking for a moment and took one of my hands. 'Even the information you receive is curated. The newspapers, well, they report very little. So much is embargoed. You will get a sense of it when the telegrams start turning up at the estate.'

'Three of the men who went will not be returning,' I said. 'We have had our share of casualties.'

'It will be much more than that. Letters are being delayed while the army is scrabbling around to find more commanding officers. They are using boys of eighteen and nineteen to lead at the front. Their heads are filled with the principles learned at public schools, but it doesn't protect them from getting their brains blown out.'

He was as emotionally volatile as I had ever seen him. I gently took back my hand, and began to walk again, hoping the motion would calm the intensity of his feelings. 'We have always agreed that war is a last resort. That it takes lives that should not be lost. That it scars all whom it touches.'

'But they can't stop it!' Fitzroy's voice rose loud enough to frighten a pheasant from the bush. He apologised immediately.

'I understand now why you did not want to have this conversation in the house.'

'I am not as in control of myself as I would like,' he said much more quietly.

'I wonder if your experiences have not affected your thoughts – and even your actions,' I said tentatively, for this was close to insulting to a spymaster.

To my utter surprise he rejoined, 'You may be right, but I also have set things in motion that cannot now be stopped.'

Everything fell into place in an instant. I had been a fool. I should have seen it. I stopped, rooted to the spot as firmly as any tree. 'You have not told Morley your plan.'

'No.'

'Then we have no resources to draw on.'

'The financial help is there as I promised.'

'But we have no one but each other!'

'I know,' said Fitzroy. 'That's the unforgivable part of it, but you are the only one I trust.'

'You've always said that you believed the purpose of espionage was to prevent or stop conflict. Is that what you hope the others – the ones in foreign services – believe too?'

I trembled from head to foot as I said this. The audacity of his plan was unspeakable. At best we would be dismissed from the service. At worst, shot for allying with the enemy.

'You are following my orders. This conversation never happened.'

'That is not a defence I would ever use,' I snapped.

'They will be as much at risk as us. No one will speak about what happens here.'

'Unless they have told their commanding officers! And have concluded this is a wonderful way to play the foolish English!'

Fitzroy looked down at his feet. 'It's in motion now.'

'I didn't want to bring the war here.'

Fitzroy sighed. 'White Orchards has been a haven for me as well. I promise I will never again bring our work to your door. My word.'

'You are putting everything I care about in danger!'

'I am,' said the spymaster. 'But too many men are dying. It is a war of attrition. It has to be stopped.'

'And you think you can do that? Your hubris will destroy us all.'

'I sincerely hope not,' said Fitzroy. 'I'm sorry, Alice. I couldn't think of another way to make things right. It is an audacious plan, but it has a chance to work – if you don't tell Morley or . . .'

'You make me complicit.'

'I had to do it.'

'I will not reveal your scheme. From now on we plan together. There will be no more surprises. You must tell me everything.'

'Thank you, Alice.'

The sunset over the field must have been glorious. I could see little of it through my tear-filled eyes. I turned to him. 'I will never forgive you for this.'

Fitzroy's head hung even lower. 'I didn't expect you would.'

We walked on for an hour into the gathering night, but there was no companionable conversation. Of the three of us, only Jack was content.

Chapter Four

Hans is up to Something

The first person to arrive for the house party, two weeks later, was one of the last people I expected to see: my brother-in-law, Hans. Bertram and I had progressed from 'pass the salt' to saying a cold 'good morning' over breakfast. We were not a happy household.

I happened to be in the hall when Hans arrived, looking for a lost box of candles. He came through the door sporting the largest box of chocolates I had ever seen. A gust of cold air carried his cologne before him. It was exquisite. His blond hair shone in the weak winter light, and his blue eyes sparkled. As usual his attire was pin-sharp perfect and showed off his elegant physique. What quite spoiled it for me was his smile, which told me he knew how good he looked. He swooped in and kissed me on the cheek. 'Merry Christmas!' he cried and handed me the box. It is worth noting that I do not particularly enjoy sweet treats.

I looked behind him and saw our new maid struggling with his luggage. 'I see Richenda didn't pack lightly,' I said with a smile.

'Ah, didn't Fitzroy tell you? She's not with me. I wasn't happy bringing the children with us, and Richenda would not come without them.' He gave me a mock salute. 'But I am here and ready to do your bidding.'

I pinned a smile on my face. 'So you know all about this.' I raised an eyebrow.

'I've been told what I need to know, apparently.' He leaned in and whispered in my ear, 'but I am your *asset*, so if you want to tell me more?'

'We'll talk later,' I said, mentally picturing getting Fitzroy in a corner and threatening him until he told me what he had tasked Hans to do.

'Fair enough,' said Hans. 'Mrs T, going to lead me to my quarters? I'm hoping I am early enough to get a good bunk!'

My housekeeper, who had been alerted to the early arrival of our first guest, blushed as most women did when Hans focused his attention on them, and led him away. He turned back for a moment as he reached the end of the hall. 'Fitzroy did tell you about – you know what, didn't he? Very sporting of you, Euphemia.' He touched the brim of his hat in salute. Goodness, was he brought up in a barn? No gentleman should keep a hat on inside the house. Hans was a loose cannon in so many ways.

I hid my concern and smiled in return. He nodded, apparently satisfied. My mental image of finding Fitzroy now included something long and pointed. Giles told me that 'Mr Fitzroy was outside with his animal.' I was impressed by the amount of scorn he was able to pour into a standard phrase. I shrugged on one of Bertram's capes and headed out.

I found Fitzroy on the back lawn playing with his dog. It was cold enough that he wore a thick tweed coat and leather gloves. Jack simply bounced to stay warm. 'Want to try your arm?' he called. 'Jack doesn't think much of my throws.' He arced a small leather ball high into the air and far along the lawn. Jack set off at a cracking pace and was back with it before I had reached Fitzroy's side. 'Goes like the clappers, doesn't he?' said his master admiringly.

'Hans has arrived.'

'Ah, yes,' said Fitzroy, bending down to pat his pet. 'I know he can be a bit much, but he's of great use at a shindig like this.'

'How?' I said coldly.

Fitzroy straightened and looked me in the eye. 'For much the same reason that you took him on as an asset, I presume. He's almost as charming as myself and his wits are somewhat above average. Besides, now he's here, you and Bertram will actually have to talk to each other. Look damned odd otherwise.'

I couldn't argue with this. 'But what is the other thing you arranged with him?'

'Ah, yes, that. I shouldn't worry about it. I doubt it will come to anything. I needed to give him a little sweetener to come.'

'Fitzroy,' I said warningly.

'He's early though. That's good. We can brief him together. After all, the whole thing with people not coming under their real names is easy enough to understand. The next part, that they are coming in small groups posing as family and relations, but may actually *be* family and relations, and that we expect only one from each group to actually be a spy, that's a bit more complicated.'

'What?'

'Oh, come on, Euphemia. You must have realised that this plan could only work if we treated it as a masquerade. Nobody is entirely sure who anyone else is. Except for me, of course. They all know of me by name. It will be rather a Christmas treat for them to meet me.'

Jack jumped up at me with muddy paws, leaving a long streak on Bertram's cape. I took the ball from between his teeth and threw it.

'Jolly good throw,' said my maddening partner.

'I had a small brother to play with when I was young.'

'Ah yes, Joe. I expect he wasn't too different from a dog.' From anyone else this might have been an insult, but Fitzroy admired most dogs more than he admired most men. He gave me a rare genuine smile.

'Oh, come on, Euphemia,' he said again. 'You can't still be cross with me. You must admit this is all going to be the most outrageous fun. And why, we might even help bring the hostilities to a conclusion. Cheer up, old girl. It's Christmas.'

Chapter Five

The Guests

Over the next two days the guests all managed to arrive when they were least expected. It felt like there was a silent competition between them to see who could arrive at the most inconvenient moment. As Fitzroy had predicted they came in little groups. Possibly the relationships between them were real, possibly not, but all of them played their parts to perfection. In all we ended up with twenty-one people in total. It transpired that Fitzroy included a 'no-later-than' clause in the invitation, so that when we sat down to dinner on the evening of the thirteenth that would be the definitive party.

The diners were:
  Fitzroy
  Bertram
  Myself
  Hans
Mr and Mrs Gruber, a young couple in their early thirties. I had met them on arrival. He was a little loud, but she was blond and sweet and spoke excellent English.
Baron von Nacht, travelling alone. I surmised he was in his thirties, and that his name was an attempt to be humorous. Undoubtedly handsome, tall and with thick dark hair, he was a pale man with intense brown eyes, who dressed predominantly in black. If he had added a cape, I would have thought him a fan of the opera. If he had added a *red* cape to his ensemble, I would have thought him a fan of

Mr Stoker. He used a silver-topped cane and seemed to pride himself on walking silently. It was all a bit too much.

The improbably named, and rather stout, Mr and Mrs Smith with their three sons. They pronounced their name as if it had a 'z' in it. Fitzroy reckoned they had thought themselves too important and brought a bodyguard. The boys, though dressed to look younger, were all between eighteen and twenty, and of rather similar features. In the end I never learned to tell one from another.

Two sisters, Mimi and Gertrude, who refused to give a surname, much like Fitzroy did. They were dressed as older ladies in too many ruffles and frills, but I observed their make-up was overthick, and I wondered about their true appearance. They spoke at length in loud whispers about whether or not their cat, Fritz, would be well enough cared for in their absence.

Lucinda Scarlatti, an extremely beautiful and glamorous woman, who was clearly Italian. I caught both Bertram and Fitzroy looking at her when they thought she wouldn't notice. With the latter it came as no surprise, but my husband is not one easily affected by beauty. Lucinda had a lovely speaking voice and moved with natural grace. I was fairly sure she was an assassin.

Charles 'Charlie' Bingham, who would clearly have been more at home selling from a London barrow. I thought he was probably one of ours, but neither he nor Fitzroy acknowledged one another, which of course meant nothing.

Winifred Mansfield, a very English name for a middle-aged woman, who spoke with a German accent, and carried her knitting everywhere. I silently vowed to ensure I kept an eye on that knitting bag and those needles.

Colonel Mathew Long and his adjunct Lieutenant Jerry Wools, who had almost comically correct military bearing. Were they perhaps making fun of us as hosts?

Ruby Milton, undoubtedly a lady, discreetly but elegantly dressed with a well-modulated voice and manners so perfect it was doubtful she was English.

John Groats, wearing a waistcoat so brash he could only be American.

Bertram was in fine fettle, and it took all my powers of persuasion to talk him out of wearing a fez to dinner as his personal disguise. (Yes, as Fitzroy had predicted, matters overtook my annoyance with him.) I dressed to look my best and concealed about my person a knife and a small revolver. I didn't often carry a gun, as Fitzroy tended to disapprove of them, but I felt this time my caution was justified. At least until I felt more comfortable among these people – if I ever did.

I headed down early to check the dinner arrangements were on course, and that neither Fitzroy nor Bertram were making a nuisance of themselves with the staff.

The dinner Mrs Warburton had arranged was quite magnificent: from mock turtle soup through goose with peas to a final course of crêpes suzette, which I feared Fitzroy might try to do himself. I had also insisted on fresh fruit, and an ice to be served for those who were not inclined to try the flaming dessert. Fitzroy and Bertram might have tried to decide the menus, but I was lady of this house.

There was also a magnificent array of side dishes from the essential roast potatoes to asparagus tossed in a light butter sauce, sausages wrapped in pastry (that Bertram so loved), dressed carrots, and some kind of offal dish Fitzroy had requested. I suspected he hoped no one would eat it and he could give it to Jack, who enjoyed such fare.

Our kitchen table fairly sagged under the strain of all the food, and to think we would be serving up at least another three such dinners! Where on earth was all this food coming from? Surely Fitzroy hadn't been able to shift produce across the country from wherever his estate or estates lay. Earlier I had seen him and Bertram huddled over some crates that I had assumed contained yet more wine. Could it have been food?

I complimented Mrs Warburton on her cooking and reassured

her that I was certain the night would be a great success. In fact, I was not sure of this at all. Then I went to do a final check on the dining room. Our butler was superb, but there are some things a hostess must see for herself.

The room was lit by candles. There was a roaring fire in the hearth. In other houses this might have been too extreme for the diners, but White Orchards had more draughts than a set of chequers. If there was a place where one surface touched another then it was certain a draught whistled through. A great deal of greenery had been placed about the room, and one of the staff had added in some red velvet bows. It was all very festive. If our guests had been any people other than spies I imagine I would have been enjoying myself a great deal. Perhaps Fitzroy was right, and I should host a dinner for the neighbours. Perhaps at New Year? After the servants' dance.

I met Fitzroy as I was exiting the room. He had come from the larger saloon where the guests were having pre-dinner drinks.

'Not as many as you feared, Alice,' said Fitzroy, rubbing his hands in glee, 'but the cream of the crop, old girl. Cream of the crop.'

'If you call me old girl once more I shall brain you with a goose!'

'I do love a good goose,' said the spy. 'Your cook does wonders with them. Hit me with a frying pan or some such if you must. Don't waste the food. I'm just going to decant a couple of decent clarets.'

'Don't tempt me,' I muttered, walking off to collect the guests. In short order I returned in formal promenade (although it was near-impossible to determine the guests' ranking, and I more or less let them sort themselves out) to my seat at the foot of the table, opposite Bertram. I had worried Fitzroy would want to be at the head, but he seemed more than happy to be seated halfway down with a lovely lady on either side, Lucinda and Ruby. Although there was a range of accents around the table, it seemed by mutual unspoken agreement that the language of the party was to be English, to the extent that everyone seemed determined to pretend they *were* English.

I heard Fitzroy give a laugh loud enough that it paused the

conversation so his next comment rang out clearly: 'I don't know, some of my most exciting times have been under the covers!' Lucinda reacted as only a foreign woman might, without a blush, but Ruby bit her lip and lowered her eyes. Perhaps she wasn't as well born as she was pretending, but one of the middle classes who were more protective of their morals. Although I did not approve, I was quite used to Fitzroy being outrageous. In some ways he was like a little boy. He loved provoking people.

I had yet to work out who all these people represented. The baron reminded me of Fitzroy. They were around the same age, and he was currently whispering in young Mrs Gruber's ear. She had gone a fetching shade of pink, while her husband had already finished his glass of wine and was calling for more. He paid her and Baron von Nacht no attention. Perhaps, I thought, they were not married at all. Fitzroy and I had pretended to be a married couple on more than one occasion with no real impropriety occurring. Dammit, but I needed to have a conversation with Fitzroy and determine who all these people were. If he even knew.

A waiter came in answer to Gruber's call and I choked on my sip of water so badly that Colonel Long had to pat me rather too firmly on the back. For an awful moment I thought I was going to spit up across the table. The footman looked across, alarmed by the noise I was making, tripped and poured a quantity of wine over Gruber, who jumped to his feet shouting. Even I, dunce as I am with languages, determined more than one French swearword. The footman was apologising and dabbing with a linen napkin. Fortunately, our inimitable butler, whose eyes were closed to all unrequired matters and open to all things necessary, sprang into action, banishing the footman before Gruber could land a punch and leading the offended gentleman from the room to change. All the while he muttered platitudes to the soaked man. The footman legged it as soon as he was given a chance, but not without throwing a horrified glance at myself. I did not meet his eye but rather turned to thank the colonel and assured him I was perfectly fine.

'Staying in position, what? Any other lady would no doubt be resting in her boudoir. Good show, what!' he said and patted my knee. My fingers clenched around my fork as I thought where I would like to stick it in him. But he released my leg at once and applied himself to his plate with far greater interest than he had shown in me.

'Ah,' echoed Fitzroy's baritone along the table. 'We've hardly begun and already there is excitement. What can come next?' He raised his glass. 'Ladies and gentlemen, a toast to our great endeavour and a curse on all clumsy footmen!'

Glasses were raised. The toast was given and there was much good-natured chuckling. I was not laughing, and I saw opposite me Bertram had assumed a grim expression. Fitzroy might not be sitting at the head of the table, but he was behaving as if he owned the place. But then Bertram had not acted to divert attention from my reaction. A reaction I would not have had if only he had told me that Barnabas Willoughby, a junior spy, who was suffering severely from shell shock, had been placed undercover as a footman. A role that would see him carrying the very best of my china and the very best of our wines. I scowled at Fitzroy, but though he caught my glance, he merely raised his glass to me. 'Better, Mrs Stapleford? You should have some wine. I've always held that water is bad for the digestion.'

Apparently I was not even to be introduced as Alice. Bertram and I were merely country folk providing the venue. I could have thrown my potatoes at him. (And I dearly like a roast potato.)

Chapter Six

The Unexpected Guest

I had more or less composed myself when Mrs T presented herself at my right ear. It is almost unheard of for a housekeeper to enter the dining room when a feast is in play. I bent my head to hear better, expecting that the cook had burned the pudding or Jack had got among the cheese.

'There is another guest, ma'am,' she said.

'Oh, how annoying. Do we have space?'

'We do, ma'am, but it seems she is not interested in her own room.'

I looked around the table. 'Is she Mrs Muller?'

'If only she were, ma'am,' said Mrs T, and I saw she was actually wringing her hands.

I pushed back my chair. 'I will come.' Clearly the matter was of such a delicate nature that the solid Mrs T could not face it. I excused myself to the colonel, 'A domestic matter,' and smiled warmly at Bertram to indicate he need not be alarmed. As Mrs T and I left, Jack darted past us and into the room. My housekeeper turned to chase after him. 'Let him go,' I said. 'Fitzroy will have a much better chance of catching him than us. Besides, he is meant to be keeping that animal under control.'

Mrs T looked a bit surprised. We all loved Jack, but at this moment I did not love Fitzroy and wanted him to know it. 'Who is it that has arrived?'

'She says Mr Frederick knows she is coming, and that she is his new wife.'

'We don't have a Mr Frederick,' I said as we reached the end of the hall. I paused outside the morning room where unexpected guests were generally corralled.

'I know, ma'am,' said Mrs T, blushing. 'At first I thought she had come to the wrong house.'

'That seems most likely. I am sure one of us can drive her back to the station.'

'But when we got into a proper discussion, ma'am, I realised she meant Mr Muller!' Mrs T wrung her hands. 'What has that foreign gentleman gone and done? Is it Continental practice to have more than one wife?'

'In the Far Eastern countries, perhaps, but not in Europe. I believe I know who this personage is. Do not fear, Mrs T, I will send her packing.'

'Is she an opportunist?'

'Indeed, I am afraid so,' I said. 'I do not believe Mr Muller has committed bigamy, whatever she may say.' I opened the door and saw the lady in question. It was who I had imagined. Esmeralda, a self-described young war widow who had pursued Hans enthusiastically across Scotland during my last mission. Hans had not been unencouraging. I entered the room and closed the door behind me.

The young woman I had previously met had been extremely pretty, but dressed in black and with a depressed air due to her supposed widowhood. The woman awaiting me in the small salon eclipsed the previous version by a country mile. She wore a bright-red coat trimmed with fur. She had undone it and beneath was an evening gown, also red, but cut to such perfection it was almost like a second skin. Her alabaster skin rose from the low-cut bodice that only just covered her with modesty. Her eyelashes were blacked with mascara, and her lips and cheeks rouged. It had been well done to enhance her natural features, and perhaps a man would not have realised the falseness. I, however, saw an artist's hand at work. She was dressed for dinner.

'My apologies for my lateness, Euphemia. You are quite out of the way here. I did not realise how far I had to travel. Of course, the snow has not helped. I hope you have all your provisions here. I imagine within the hour we will be quite snowed in.'

I heard this with a sinking heart. 'Esmeralda,' I said. 'I had not looked to see you at this gathering. It is linked to my husband's business affairs. Our family Christmas celebrations will not begin for some weeks. It was to that I believe Hans had foolishly issued you an invitation?'

'Foolishly?'

'I presume you have been in correspondence with him?'

'Indeed.'

'And as an intelligent woman you must have realised he is married?'

She put her hand against a chairback. I thought for one moment she was about to attempt a swoon. 'Come, come!' I said. 'You have already acknowledged him by his given name, Hans, and not the alias he gave you.'

The hand stayed in situ, but the lady's back straightened. She turned her gaze directly on me. 'Come, come, Euphemia!' she said. 'Is it not possible that Hans Muller wishes to be rid of his cumbersome wife and children and to return to a more London life? He is a financial genius, and he is rotting away in the country.'

'He has German antecedents and is lucky he is not interned in a camp!'

'Indeed. Why is that?'

'His father was German and his mother was a lover of all things German.'

'Are you not through your grandmother closely related to the royal family, who are all of German descent, and I believe speak German among themselves? And yet no one seeks to lock you up. Instead, it seems you are most trusted by the realm.'

'This is not to the point,' I said, attempting to model myself on my mother, who had in her time made a duke cry through sheer authority. 'It has nothing to do with your presence here.'

She walked towards the window, and pulled back the curtain. The room was low-lit enough that I could see the flurry of snow falling. 'Will you turn me out to walk in this on foot, as my conveyance has gone, and carrying my own luggage? I brought a trunk.'

She finished as if this clinched the matter. I liked her less and less by the minute, but it would have taken a harder heart than mine to toss her out into the elements. Besides, for a time Hans and I had worried she was an enemy agent. We later assured ourselves she was not, but perhaps we had been wrong and we would have to shoot her after all. This idea, though I knew it to be fantasy, cheered me a little.

'No, I will not turn you out in this, but neither will I ask my staff to escort you to Hans Muller's bedroom when they know he is married to my sister-in-law. We are a moral household. I will ask my housekeeper to find somewhere else for you to sleep.'

'You may wish to bear in mind that Fitzroy is expecting me.'

A whisper of an earlier conversation came back to me. Hans saying something about my being 'a good sport' and Fitzroy telling me to pay no attention. Would he really have dared condone such a tryst under my and Bertram's roof? It seemed too far even for him. But the satisfied smile on Esmeralda's face, which I heartily wished to slap, indicated that she thought she had me in a bind.

'You have been misled,' I said, 'if you believe that this house is under either the auspices of Hans Muller or Fitzroy. Bertram Stapleford is the master here and he will not countenance such immorality. I will have you escorted to a room. It will be smaller than I would normally give a guest, but we are extremely full. You may join us for the rest of dinner, but any suggestion that you are here as Hans's fiancée or paramour and my husband will have no qualms in throwing you out into the blizzard.' I turned on my heel and stormed out of the room.

The situation had moved from a minor annoyance to one that had me pushing down a roaring rage. It was not merely the audaciousness of Hans and Fitzroy's actions, inexcusable as they were, but also that they both well knew the situation would disturb my invalid husband. Bertram might look his good self tonight, but he hid a weak heart and disabled system.

I gave my orders to Mrs T and returned to the dining room. I smiled at my husband as I reseated myself. The diners were still on the entrée and I quickly summoned a footman to provide me with more roasted potatoes and asparagus. I managed to catch Fitzroy's eye as I was helping myself to a few spears and threw him such an angry look that the affected monocle he was wearing this evening fell out of his eye and down into his gravy. Hans ducked my gaze. Signally, he clearly knew what had occurred.

It was not many moments later that Esmeralda swept into the room. All eyes went to her, not merely due to her swift entrance, but also due to her gown which rode as close to the line of decency as I have ever seen. Even my husband gaped. The atmosphere in the room grew noticeably colder as every woman, young or mature, threw her a frosty look. All of us women knew there was only one reason to wear such a dress in the country – or indeed anywhere else: it was not merely designed to attract a man's attention but to seduce. It seemed even female spies can be scandalised. Young Mrs Gruber, who had been rejoined by her husband in the time I was absent, adeptly nipped her husband's wrist to refocus his attention on herself. Hans had half risen from his seat, and stayed thus like the insect that he was, pinned under my gaze.

Quietly, I directed the footman nearest to me to put a chair at the table where there was a slight gap between the spinster Mimi and Lieutenant Wools. It would mess up the order of the table, but the Grubers, by insisting on being seated together, had already done that. I left the space because it necessitated the diner having their back directly in front of the roaring fire. It was also the only place to put another diner without incommoding the others. However, the situation made me smile sweetly as I gestured Esmeralda over to the place. I flung an angry glance at Hans, who sat down again as quickly as if he had been shot. Fitzroy was calmly cleaning his monocle on his napkin and did not look my way for the rest of the meal. It did not matter. I meant to corner him afterwards.

Chapter Seven

After-Dinner Conversation

Of course, after the meal the women had to withdraw. I led the ladies to a refreshment of tea and tiny cakes in the drawing room. The gentlemen would have port over the remains of the table, but I rather feared Fitzroy and Bertram would lead them away to the smoking room or the billiard room, where I could not enter this evening – due to the ridiculous rigours of social etiquette. Although I did wonder if these held sway among a group of spies.

Mimi and Gertrude asked for whisky with their petits fours. Mrs Gruber requested a sweet sherry. Lucinda and Ruby took Esmeralda aside and began a swift and complicated game of cards with her which would quickly fleece her of any monies she had brought with her. Esmeralda played happily, and out of the corner of my eye I saw she was much more adept than I had thought. The losses and gains between them were fairly even.

I was captured, there is no other word for it, by Winifred Mansfield, a woman of indeterminate age that rested on the wrong side of the childbearing years. I had seen that she had brought an unusually large bag into dinner. This turned out not to be the holder of a pistol, which I might have expected, but of a weapon more formidable. It was another knitting bag containing several balls of yarn, knitting needles and various pieces of work in progress. I was barely halfway through my first cup of tea when I found myself holding wool for her to wind.

'You are most kind, Baroness,' she said in a thick accent. It sounded vaguely German to me, which meant she was most likely from Austria nearby.

'Not at all,' I replied as if holding wool was the most delightful thing I could have done with my evening. 'I hope you enjoyed your dinner.' I did not remark on her using a title that was still in debate after the death of Bertram's older brother and which my husband despised.

'You do not mind I use your title?' she asked as if reading my mind.

'No,' I said.

'Your husband I think does not like such things.' She lowered her voice. 'If the likes of Mimi and Gertrude are to be believed then to think such things or act upon them will become most unwise.'

Spies, I thought, they must always hint at secrets. It was so tiresome. A little straight talking could have so many things sorted in short order. But neither sovereigns nor their secret services, I had learned, had the habit of laying their cards on the table, despite what was happening with Esmeralda. I heard her give a little squeal of happiness as she won a trick. I winced. 'I will bear it in mind,' I said to Winifred.

'I hope I am wrong,' said Winifred. 'The world it is changing too fast. Queen Victoria hoped by marrying her children into all the royal families she felt of significance to achieve a legacy. I have always presumed that she hoped they would also live in peace. Do you think so?'

Dammit! This was like playing at charades. Until we had established who was representing which country one had no idea about motivations and meanings. I really hoped that Fitzroy had some cunning way to sort things out tomorrow. As it was, I had the distinct impression that all the other spies were enjoying this strange masquerade immensely. I hadn't wanted to kick Fitzroy this hard for a long time.

Esmeralda's laugh floated by again. At least I knew about the motivations of one individual. How I was to pull Hans out of his mess I had no idea. I would only consider helping him for the sake of his wife. Otherwise, I'd happily have turned them both out into the snow.

'So how do you think?'

'Oh, my apologies, the winding of the wool is quite mesmeric, is it not?' I said, hedging for time.

'I assume that is where the term wool-gathering comes from?'

'Quite possibly. I was not raised in the way of domestic minutiae,' I said, reddening slightly. 'My mother, you see, always thought I would end up marrying a man with a great house and that I would need to understand how such is run.'

Winifred cast her eye about the salon. It was nicely furnished, but hardly more than a decent country drawing room.

I gave a little laugh. 'Not a house like this. I married for love. Not for fortune.'

Winifred gave me a sombre nod. 'Much wiser and not I think the way of your late queen's children.'

'You are correct in thinking that she was most keen on bloodlines and felt that hers and Albert's combined would be the best for Europe and the surrounding countries. Whether or not she thought it would bring peace, I do not know. But it is quite traditional to cement alliances with marriage.'

'And yet her grandson seeks her throne.'

I hadn't heard anyone say this quite as boldly before, but I had to remember who I was with.

'I have wondered if it is merely because he thinks he could do it the best. He would never, of course, be accepted by the British public. We would see riots in the street and revolution before he took the throne,' I claimed confidently.

'We will, I believe, see revolution in the Austro-Hungarian Empire before long. The new Emperor may hope to broker a peace, but I fear he is not long for his throne. He has recently reintroduced feudalism in the hope it will contain his people. You are still quite feudal here, are you not?'

'Noblesse oblige remains a guiding light, but the forces of industry are creating another stratum of the population.'

'A middle class.'

'That has been growing for some time. No, I was referring to the arrival of industrial barons and the influence they are beginning to wield.'

'These times make such men a great deal of money.'

'Yes, I fear they must be soulless to profit so,' I said thoughtfully.

'Perhaps,' said Winifred, 'but men are always the better for the wise counsel of their women. Here, the wool is done. Thank you for your assistance. I shall detain you no longer. You have, no doubt, many matters to attend to this evening. If I may be permitted to give you one further piece of advice?'

'Of course,' I said.

'Do not stand on social mores among the likes of us. Do what you must. It is what such as we are for.' She nodded at me, and I found myself on my feet before I realised, as if I had been kindly dismissed by a headmistress.

I walked to the door thinking intensely. Fitzroy, by dint of his wider travels and knowledge of languages, tended to be the one who would familiarise me with an overview of the world when necessary. But generally our missions were precise and focused on a small group of individuals and the interplay of emotions and motivations between them. It was there I excelled. Although I had recently discovered that arranging the necessities of troops, from food to possible escape exits, was not dissimilar to the skills required to run a Great House. They were at least related and I felt I had become good at exploiting this similarity.

As I walked away from my new friend, I had the impression that Winifred had tried to impart a great deal to me, and I had been too uninformed to gather it all. Damn Fitzroy and Bertram for being so obtuse. If we had been able to talk together before this event I might have been better prepared. It was, after all, entirely their faults I had not been talking to them.

I left the room in search of Fitzroy. My desire to kick him further increased.

Chapter Eight

On the Lawn

The hallway was deserted. I could hear the sounds of male laughter from behind closed doors, most of it hearty, but with the occasional bray of the American. Fitzroy was dreaming if he thought the Americans would give us more help than they already had. The bray came again. It had to be John Groats, surely a most crude pseudonym. At least Esmeralda and Hans were being kept apart for now.

I heard a soft step behind me and turned instantly. The impossibly named Baron von Nacht, handsome, smartly dressed and with a faint smile on his lips, stood before me. I had no idea where he had come from. I had heard no door close. He stepped forward and took my hand. He bent over and kissed it. I watched as if outside myself, bemused and not unappreciative of his startling dark-haired beauty and fine masculine features. 'I did not wish to alarm you,' he said in a low, well-modulated tone. I felt my heart beat a little faster.

I gave myself a mental shake. 'You did not,' I replied. 'I have a number of things on my mind.'

He had straightened but still held my hand. 'And yet you responded with alacrity to the slight sound I made. Bravo! It is wise to be cautious when one is among a nest of snakes. Even when one is a snake oneself.' He gave me a wide smile, and before I knew it had tucked my hand under his arm. 'Let us walk together a little. I would suggest the garden, but the snow falls ever faster.'

'I do not think the flurries are so strong. I can collect my cape from the hall. Our footsteps will chaperone us,' I said, smiling.

'Fitzroy had told me you were remarkable. Yet, I think, for once, he has underplayed his hand.'

We collected capes and galoshes and stepped out on the back lawn. The snow lay flat and perfect. Our shoes sank a good few inches and left perfect imprints. 'Ah,' said von Nacht, 'I see what you mean. It will be clear where we have walked and how we have stood.'

'Until it snows again at any rate.' I looked up at the sky. It remained pregnant with snow. This was merely a break in the blizzard.

'You are also very lovely,' said the baron. 'My compliments do not distress you, do they?'

'I think most women enjoy appropriate attention,' I said.

'I have been warned to behave myself. Although I must confess such a command coming from our mutual acquaintance made me laugh a great deal at the time.'

'Baron, if you mean to imply—'

'Please call me Alex, and I mean to imply nothing where you are concerned. It was seeing Fitzroy play the moral man that had me in stitches. I am aware he has nothing but the proudest respect for you. I also spent some time playing billiards with your husband tonight. A remarkable mind he has. I think he is one of the most politically aware men of his generation. I have no doubt Fitzroy is terribly jealous.'

I did not rise to the bait to answer him. Instead I took in our surroundings. A little light was spilling from the house, and the moon, shy tonight, still lent a little creamy glitter to the garden. I found it entrancing. Moonlight and snow is one of nature's most beautiful combinations. 'It is hard to imagine the suffering amongst all this beauty.'

'Indeed, a war conducted from the drawing rooms of European royalty and their generals can seem more like a game to many. The group Fitzroy and I have gathered here are all personally aware of the action on the front lines, either from personal experience or by hearing about it first hand from someone they value. In some things I agree with your partner that one of the roles of espionage is to curtail war, as much as it is to prevent war during peacetime.'

'So you believe there must be a push for peace?' I tried not to react to the news that he believed he had planned this occasion with Fitzroy. He, too, was looking out at the beauty around us, so he might have missed my reaction.

'Of course. But regular channels have had no success. So it is time for the irregular,' he said.

'Who do you think to reach and with what message?'

Alex shook his head. We had reached the end of the lawn, and he turned to me. Looking down into my eyes, his were nothing but black in this light and I had a sensation of looking into an abyss. Naturally dark, unlike Fitzroy who must generally dye his red hair, I assessed that Alex was the more handsome. What havoc the two of them could wreak across the female gentility of Europe.

'I represent Charles the First, the Austro-Hungarian Emperor. He seeks to bring both sides to the table to end this ridiculous war.'

'He is afraid that his empire is not as strong as he might wish?'

'Perhaps,' said Alex. 'Times are uncertain. But the Ottoman Empire will fall before ours.'

I really didn't know enough about this, so I tried to look wise. 'How does your Emperor intend to go about this?'

'Obviously, he does not know what I intend to do.' He turned, and with my hand still tucked in his arm I perforce followed him as he began to walk the width of the lawn. 'Fitzroy and I have spoken in vague terms, but I suppose it is time to come to the point – at least as far as you are concerned. We are determined to get the Kaiser and the King together to discuss their differences.'

'I doubt very much they will agree!' I said, startled that this plan should be so simple.

'Oh, neither of us is under any delusions about their various exaltednesses' desire to meet.'

'Then how?' I stopped. Alex was pulled backwards towards me, but he overcame this with grace. He gestured gracefully, 'You must know there is only one way.'

'No,' I said. 'You could not. He would not.'

'We have both seen the horror of the front line. It cannot continue. The waste of life is unconscionable. Your husband has the sort of brain to create a peace plan. I am surprised Fitzroy has not already tasked him with it.'

'But how do you mean to get them together?'

'A little subterfuge.'

'Subterfuge!' I almost shouted. 'You mean to kidnap them both and force them to negotiate.'

'Fitzroy said you were sharp, and so you can see we have no choice. Both are intent on the war.'

'You expect to gain the agreement of everyone here?' I gestured back at the house.

'I am unsure. This part was Fitzroy's plan. He said that if the services could send representatives who might speak without being identified then they might be prepared to entertain the idea. Make no mistake, for all I am working for my Emperor, this is a plan made among spies, by spies and for spies to enact.'

'You will all be shot for treason!'

'I very much hope not. While we wear our virtual masks of anonymity we have the cape of plausible deniability.'

'Perhaps so, but not when you act!'

'If it ends the war, I believe there will be more rejoicing than anger. Again, this is an occasion for each to discover what would informally be acceptable to another nation to end their part in this madness.'

I pulled my hand away. 'Yes. Yes. I quite see what you are trying to do. I think this is not only dangerous but misguided.'

'I would challenge the misguided label, but is not what we do always dangerous?'

'But we serve,' I protested. 'We serve our rulers and our countries. We do not—'

'Take charge? Perhaps it is time we did.' There was a steeliness in his tone that suggested any confrontation would not be well met. Time and events had pushed him to the edge of his conscience and he was acting from the heart. Men can be so passionately foolish.

'I think I need some time to think about all this. You need not be concerned that I will expose your plan before you have talked to the others – or indeed told anyone outside this snowbound circle.' As I said this a few flakes of snow fluttered down on our heads. I looked up at the sky and said, 'Indeed we should return inside. I believe the blizzard is starting again.'

Alex took my hand once more and bowed over it. 'Indeed. Talk with Fitzroy; he will perhaps explain the situation better than I. But know this: I stand here as an ally to you both.'

I smiled in acknowledgement, but spoke no more; instead I led us back into the warm confines of the house. I had to find Fitzroy. I urgently needed to discuss matters with him.

Chapter Nine

The Close of Play for the Day

When we approached the French windows, Alex suddenly drew me back swiftly and to the side, so that we were outside the glass. Actually he swept his cloak around me, obscuring my identity, and clasping me tightly enough to his chest that I could feel the hardness of the muscles through his shirt. I did not immediately protest. I had heard the slight intake of breath before he acted. He was hiding from someone, and unless he showed me violence I would go along with this. It was warm inside his cape, and being the shorter I was almost engulfed. He smelled of cigars and cedar-sweet cologne. It was not unpleasant.

'Did you hear that?' Hans's voice, coming from inside the house. The French windows must be ajar or else whoever it was had had the same idea as us and was about to venture outside for some privacy.

'There is no one nearby,' answered Esmeralda. She sounded exasperated.

'Come outside where we can discuss things more freely?'

'In these shoes? Besides, I would have to ask the butler for my coat and your slyness would be undone.'

'I'm sure Euphemia has something lying around here you can borrow.'

'Oh yes, she would love that. The woman loathed me at first sight. Why did you ask me to come, Frederick?' She gave a sniff.

'Oh, you know why, Esmeralda. You are everything to me. I could not possibly let you go. We are twin souls. You must feel it?'

I felt Alex's body shake slightly, and realised he was laughing silently. Personally, I felt nauseous.

There was a rather unpleasant slurping sound. I realised they must be kissing.

'Come away,' said Hans in a low husky voice, 'let us find somewhere where we can be together properly. Be as one.'

I was grateful my face was hidden from Alex's sight for I felt myself blush scarlet. I had always known that Hans was unfaithful to my sister-in-law. Indeed, he had propositioned me on more than one occasion. But it had been done in quite a matter-of-fact way. This was different. He had been breathing heavily and clearly feeling quite – well – aroused at the time. Whoever Esmeralda was I could not allow him to take her as a mistress under my roof. I made to move forward, but the arm around my waist held me fast.

Alex bent to whisper softly in my ear. 'For this gathering you are a spy, not the guardian of your family's honour. Leave them to their business.'

'But,' I said, attempting to wriggle free.

'No buts,' said Alex, 'and please no squirming. It is very distracting.' He let me go then, and I hurried into the house, but of the speakers there was no sign.

As soon as we were divested of our outside clothing, Alex disappeared back into the male-occupied rooms of the house. I expected he would provide some explanation of his absence, and I decided I would use the kitchen as my excuse. There was no one in the hall to see my descent into the servants' area, and thus no one to know how long I had been out there.

I merely reassured my dear cook that everything had been wonderful before I returned upstairs and made my way to the library. There was a small room off it that Fitzroy had a way of gravitating towards. We kept the best decanted whiskies there. When the three of us were in good accord it was not uncommon for Fitzroy, Bertram and I to spend time there drinking and putting the world to rights.

I found him sitting a little way from the table, on which stood a mostly empty whisky decanter, staring into the flames of a lovely fire. Realising how cold I had become I hastened towards the heat.

'Alice!' exclaimed Fitzroy and shot out of his seat, arms wide. He embraced me and planted a kiss firmly on the top of my head. He did have the decency to let me go before I stood on his instep.

'You're drunk!'

'A bit tiddly,' he said, sitting back down, but somehow capturing one of my hands. 'You're cold. Do you want to sit on my lap?'

I pulled my hand free. 'Stop being outrageous,' I commanded. 'Whatever has got into you?'

Fitzroy leaned across the table and poured himself another drink. He sloshed a bit into another glass and handed it to me. 'Thanks for not slapping me,' he said. 'Just a bit overwhelmed. Dangerous times. Having you by my side is the one bit of reassurance I have in all this.'

I pulled out a chair and sat. 'So you are intent on this kidnapping?' His jaw actually dropped. 'The baron has been spinning me the most incredible story, is it true?'

'So you've met Alex.' He took a sip. 'Naughty man that. Best of intentions though.'

'Are you going along with this plan?'

Fitzroy hiccupped. Something I had never seen him do on alcohol before. Herring once, but not whisky. 'Not yet. Got all the spies together to see if they'll go for it.' He took another sip. 'You see only the ones that had done a fair bit of service were invited. All of us loyal to a man or woman. No traitors. No. No. That would never do. All in good service to our masters. Or at least I think so. To be entirely honest, not worked out who all of 'em are working for yet. But I will!' He took another sip and smacked his lips together in a most ungentlemanly manner.

'But what you propose to do is treasonous!'

Fitzroy blinked at me. 'That's the problem, Alice. Have to find a way it isn't. Service to Crown and Country – that's who I am. That's my life. Given up everything for it. Even you. Can't turn traitor.' He looked at the bottom of his glass. 'This damn stuff keeps evaporating.'

'I think you should go to bed,' I said. I stood and took the glass gently off him. 'We can discuss everything in the morning. Of course you could never be a traitor. And you're wrong, you haven't lost me. I'm always here as your partner. With all these spies available we must be able to come up with some scheme that will shorten the war. I have heard no one here sing its praises.'

Fitzroy stood up. 'You're right, as usual, Alice.' He patted me on the shoulder. 'Take the compliment, probably won't say that when I am sober.'

'It's not like you to—'

'Told you earlier, dear girl. Been feeling rather down. Right, off up the wooden stairs to Bedfordshire. Breakfast together? Before the others attack the kippers?'

'Yes, good idea. Good night.'

I did a quick round to ensure all my guests had what they needed. Some had already slipped away to bed. There was no sign of Esmeralda or Hans. Lucy and Ruby had gone up. I found Winifred, Mimi and Gertrude sitting around the table playing a fiendishly complicated game. Ascertaining they had all they needed I wished them good night. I could hear singing coming from the billiard room and hesitated before entering. Bertram came out. 'Effy!' he cried. His eyes were glittering with excitement and the colour on his cheeks was high. 'This has been a brilliant night, has it not? The most excellent food and the most excellent company. It has been a long time since I have been able to converse with such minds.'

As Bertram generally loathes spies, I had to assume he had been Fitzroy's drinking partner for at least some of the evening.

'Shall we retire?' I said. 'I have ascertained that the ladies still awake need nothing more. How fare the gentlemen?'

Bertram waved his arm expansively. 'They'll all be fine. Better tell old Giles to check for smoking embers though. Not all of them as accurate as one might want with the old ashtray.'

'Oh, good Lord!'

'Don't worry. It's all going to be good. Except for Hans: when Richenda hears what he's been up to he's a dead man.' He giggled at this, finding the thought amusing in his inebriated state.

'One could hardly blame her,' I said. 'He is a cad.'

Bertram began to walk carefully alongside me towards our chambers. 'It's what I've always said, Euphemia, once a cad always a cad.'

'But you are talking about Fitzroy when you say that.'

'Well, yes, him too.' He stopped. 'That's not fair. Hans is a bounder. Fitzroy would never be a bounder. Brought some jolly good wine with him and beat that von Nacht poser at billiards. Grand bloke really.'

'Von Nacht?'

'No,' exploded my husband, stumbling forward into walking once more. 'Fitzroy. I think I've been too hard on him. Grand chap. Happy to have him visit any time.'

I escorted my husband to bed, which he shortly fell into and began snoring like a walrus. This, I thought, is marriage. I settled down beside him. It felt like even my pillow was vibrating. But I did not care. I had this. Away from the world of spying I had a good man who loved me and with whom I shared a gentle civilian life. It kept me grounded. Even if his snores did keep me awake.

Chapter Ten

The Party Increases Again

I was roused in the early morning by what I at first thought was a tremendous snore from Bertram. To be fair, when he has not been drinking with Fitzroy, he snores very little. Considering how inebriated Fitzroy had allowed himself to become I had already formed the intention of greeting my beloved at luncheon and not before. He was going to have a devil of a head.

But as I lay awake, watching the grey fingers of light peep beneath our curtains, I became aware of noises beyond his snoring. It sounded as if someone had arrived downstairs. I supposed it was possible that another group was coming to join us. Fitzroy had driven Mrs T to distraction with his inability to give accurate numbers of guests. However, I had not been warned; the bed was warm, and this whole thing having been forced on me, I decided that unless I was actually summoned I could remain blissfully unaware of any new arrival. It was not what my mother had taught me, but then she had issued no strictures on how spies should be treated. I turned over and went back to sleep. This dismissal of my duty as hostess would haunt me for some time to come. I will never know if things would have gone quite differently if I had risen to the occasion.

I had drifted into a deep sleep and was dreaming of fierce seas and stormy winds when I, along with the rest of the house, was awoken by a shattering scream. Immediately I was on my feet and out of the door. Doors opened all along this landing and the next. The majority of us present were used to responding to alarm immediately. Bertram, however, did not stir behind me.

The scream had sounded alarmingly familiar, but I couldn't bear to believe it was who I thought it was. I ran towards where I thought the scream was coming from. In the middle of the west wing corridor, in front of an open door, an expression of agony on her face, I saw Richenda, Hans's wife and Bertram's sister. A woman we had all thought to be miles away preparing Christmas for her family at home. Without thinking I checked her hands for weapons, and saw none. Hans, in his (rather splendid) dressing gown, barrelled out of the door, slamming it behind him. His hair was askew, and his legs shockingly bare. He then uttered the fateful words, 'Darling, I can explain.'

About me I felt, rather than heard, the ripple of an audible sigh. I caught sight of Mimi in a hugely frilly nightdress tucking away something that looked suspiciously like a stiletto. Mrs Mansfield was also present in night attire but with her knitting bag to hand. There was no sign or Ruby or Lucy nor of Fitzroy or Alex. I tried not to draw the obvious conclusions. Mr Gruber, standing in his bedroom doorway also attired for the night, spat rather than said, 'A domestic uproar! How unprofessional!'

At this, doors all along the two hallways began to slam shut as the spies returned to their rest. I still stood frozen at the sight in front of me when I heard footsteps charging up the steps. But it wasn't Fitzroy; it was Barnabas Willoughby, ashen-faced, trembling, but clearly prepared to do his bit.

His appearance unfroze me from my shock. I had never known if Richenda was aware of Hans's infidelities. I had assumed so. It had not been a marriage for love, but one of convenience for them both. Hans was attempting to pet Richenda on the shoulder and was speaking softly to her, as she, crying, pushed him away.

'It's all right, Willoughby,' I said. 'It seems that my brother-in-law's antics have finally caught up with him. If you could find Fitzroy for me, please? This mess is of his making.'

Before Willoughby could answer I heard a sudden crack and then a thud and cry of surprise from Hans. Richenda had punched him squarely in the face.

'I told you, I am under cover,' said Hans, holding his broken nose. Blood streamed down his front.

'I know. I bloody well saw you,' shouted Richenda, her voice only slightly less loud than a judgement bell. She stormed away from him and straight into me. Willoughby took one look at the situation and bolted. I caught Richenda by the shoulders and tried to steady her.

'She surprised us last night,' I said. 'I did my best to keep them apart, but I appear to have been outwitted.'

'You knew he had a mistress?' Richenda was shaking now, and I thought it unlikely I was about to experience what was likely to be a formidable right hook.

'No,' I said. 'I have met her before by accident when we travelled to Scotland.' I glanced over at Hans and decided to throw him a tiny bone. 'It was clear she was keen to pursue him, but they had not – er – engaged in intimacies during that time. I did not invite her here and would not have done so.'

I noticed Hans's bedroom door was closed. In fact he was trying to open it with one hand while the other staunched the blood. It appeared to have been locked from the inside.

'You know her?' squeaked the indignant wife.

'Only to speak to. She attached herself to our party for a while, and we were in need of the – er – camouflage.'

'So Hans isn't lying when he says he goes to London for you?'

I wasn't prepared to go that far. 'Are the children with you?'

'Only my maid.'

'Then, if you will forgive me, I will dress. After such a shock you need a brandy and time to gather yourself. We can discuss matters later. Mrs T will take you to a room to freshen up.'

Thankfully the amazing Mrs T had appeared fully dressed and bright-eyed with curiosity. Her eyes opened wide as she recognised Richenda. She showed my sister-in-law all due deference and led her away, completely ignoring Hans.

'What on earth's the matter?' called a very grumpy-sounding Fitzroy from down the stairs. I leaned over the banister and answered as quietly as I could. 'Hans's wife has arrived and caught him in – the act.'

Fitzroy ran lightly up the steps. He looked at Hans, who having failed to get into his room was now sitting on the floor leaning against the wall looking woeful and bloody. 'The other one's locked him out,' I said.

'Good God,' said Fitzroy. 'How utterly appalling. A gentleman must be able to handle his own affairs. Who hit him?'

'Richenda.'

Fitzroy grinned. 'A lady with spirit. Better get a footman to clean him up.'

'My clothes are all inside,' said Hans. 'Esmeralda won't let me in.'

'Not my problem. Send him off with the servants, Alice, and we can chat over our early breakfast. Although I think you should probably wear more than that. Wouldn't want to upset old Bertie.'

'Old Bertie is snoring his head off and most likely going to wake up with a very sore head.' I looked accusingly at him.

'I've got a dreadful head,' said the spymaster. 'Must have been something wrong with one of the bottles I got from my father's cellar. I'll have to speak to his cellarman next time I'm there.'

'No pity,' I said shortly, and went off to dress.

When I came down, the breakfast room was bristling with guests and their chatter. Of Fitzroy there was no sign. Willoughby came up behind me. 'He's in the morning room.' I poured myself a cup of coffee and went to find him.

I found him sitting behind a generous spread. 'Enough for two!' he cried on seeing me, and with his mouth still full of toast. He passed me a clean plate.

'My staff spoil you,' I said, sitting down and beginning to help myself to dishes in front of me.

'I'm a terribly likeable fellow. Marmalade? Mrs T's special blend for Christmas, I believe?'

'Good grief, she wouldn't even let Bertram have some. She's been hoarding it for the day itself.'

'So, what shall we do about this mess in your house?' said Fitzroy.

'Unless you wish to wear that kipper you are currently inhaling I suggest you rephrase that.'

'It's a mess. It's in your house.'

'But you told Hans he could bring Esmeralda.'

Fitzroy paused with his knife in the air. 'No, you did.'

'I most certainly did not. He suggested while we were in Scotland that she join us for Christmas and I did not agree.' I took a large sip of coffee. Fitzroy instantly filled my cup. 'At the time I thought it was all part of his wooing. I had little time for it and made my disapproval clear.'

'Did you hit him too?' Fitzroy perked up.

'No, of course not.' I saw his face fall. 'I don't know why my hitting people always cheers you up.'

He flaked some fish on to a piece of toast and picked it up with his fingers. 'Look, Alice. I suspect he'll say that each of us agreed to this. Don't let it distract us any further. I am sorry for Richenda and I think Hans is a crass fool, but it's not what this weekend is all about.'

'Unless Esmeralda is some foreign spy sent to interrupt us.'

Fitzroy swallowed quickly. 'Could she be? You never did find out her surname. Shoddy work that, Alice.'

'I don't believe she is a foreign spy. I checked her background as much as I could on the road, and with Edinburgh's local service. When I returned I put it all in my report to Morley.'

'Did it occur to you to ask Hans what her full name was? Or weren't you speaking to him at the time?'

'You're being petty,' I snapped. Under the circumstances I thought I had done a decent job in Scotland. Not a perfect one, but decent. 'I did wonder about her motives at one point, but she so clearly showed herself to be a silly woman infatuated with Hans – and though I am slightly ashamed to admit it I kept her around as . . .'

'Camouflage?'

I nodded and didn't meet his eyes.

'So no flags raised on the limited information you had?'

'No,' I said. 'If anything, this all goes to prove Hans is utterly unreliable and should never be used as an asset again.'

'Pity,' said Fitzroy. 'He's a smart man when he's thinking with this head. And he's well motivated, being part German and not wanting to go into a camp. Probably won't be able to avoid that now.'

'Richenda? The children?' I said in alarm.

'No, I should think we can manage to keep them out. Richenda will have to lay off the violence though. All that can be sorted out later. We only have this one chance to have everyone together.'

'Yes, yes, but what are we going to do?'

'Ah,' whispered Fitzroy, leaning over the table so his face was close to mine, 'this is where things start to get really interesting.'

Chapter Eleven

Out of the Woodwork

Fitzroy's plan for the day was to allow the guests to mingle throughout the house and have discreet conversations. 'We're still at the masquerade stage,' he said. 'People can say what they really think without acknowledging their allegiance. Once we have some sort of overall agreement, hopefully by tomorrow, we can put an action plan together.'

'Your alarming plan. I take it that is meant to be a final, desperate measure.'

Fitzroy put down his knife and folk. 'Von Nacht really is out of order.'

'Why?'

'Because, my dear girl, that is out-and-out treason and I would never involve you in such a thing.'

'But if it stopped the war?'

'Even if it did bring peace, the notable people involved would still be well within their rights to have Alex and me shot.'

'So would you do it?'

Fitzroy upended half a jar of marmalade over his piece of thickly buttered toast. 'Honestly? I don't know. We discussed a number of alarming ideas. This gathering was the best of them all. I wonder what Alex's game is, trying to bring you in on all that? I think I should have words with him.'

'As you said to me, is this the time?'

'No, but I don't want him embroiling you in anything clandestine.'

I couldn't help but laugh at this.

'Now, Alice, when have I ever... oh well, don't answer that. But I have always been acting on behalf of King and Country.'

'Let's concentrate on how we can make this meeting yield useful fruit,' I said. 'We are certainly not going to be disturbed by anyone else. Look at the weather out there. How on earth did Richenda's carriage get through?'

Fitzroy turned his gaze to the window. 'Rather pretty, isn't it? Do you know snow actually does make things sound louder. Much harder to sneak up on someone when it's lying like this.'

'I don't know why Richenda decided to come. Do you think Hans let something slip?'

Fitzroy stood up, throwing his napkin down with unnecessary, but clearly unsatisfying, force. 'I don't bloody care. I've had enough of that little ménage à trois. Time to get to work, Alice.'

I was desperate to investigate the family situation further, but Fitzroy clearly thought this could wait, and dragged me into a session in the library with Mimi and Gertrude. 'See what you can get out of them. They're as tight as a pair of shrivelled oysters around me,' he hissed in my ear as he sidled off before I could ask him where he was going.

The two ladies were sitting looking through a copy of Bertram's first edition of *A Christmas Carol*. After ascertaining they did not mind me joining them, I said, 'I'm so sorry your sleep was disturbed this morning.'

Mimi, at least I think it was Mimi for they were uncannily alike, shrugged. 'It was no danger to any of us. That is good.'

'For one moment,' chipped in Gertrude, 'I feared the situation was to be overtaken by your police.'

'I can't imagine that happening,' I said quite truthfully. 'Our police do not concern themselves with – with – the more obscure forms of diplomacy.'

Gertrude laughed at that. 'Obscure and violent diplomacy. Sometimes the heart must be cut out for the body to flourish.'

This seemed a most unsuccessful metaphor to me, but I smiled slightly.

'This is your book?' asked Mimi.

'My husband's. He is very fond of Dickens.'

'We approve,' said Mimi. 'He writes about the real people, and this moneylender, Scrooge, is punished for how he has treated others.'

'It's one of Dickens's more moral stories,' I said.

'Ah, morality,' said Gertrude. 'Morality is born of circumstance, I think.'

'In this country, we tend to draw our morality from the Christian Bible. Church and State are closely linked.'

Mimi made a noise by sucking at her teeth. 'You do not agree?' I asked.

'The Bible is all about sharing and compassion. I do not see much of this here. You, for instance, have the most lovely house, but it requires the servitude of many to work your house and gardens for you to have the way of life you enjoy.'

'We pride ourselves that all our employees are well treated and happy in their roles,' I said carefully. I was fairly sure now I was talking to representatives, not of the Tsar, but one of the rising combative elements in Russia.

'If they came to you and said they were unhappy, what would you do?'

'Ask them how I could make things better, and if I could not,' I added, forestalling Mimi, 'I would find them a better position elsewhere.'

We continued to fence with words for a while. When I relayed my conversation to Fitzroy in the little library shortly before luncheon, he agreed with me. 'Interesting. I don't think we have anyone representing the Tsar here. That the Bolsheviks should bother to attend surprises me. In some ways it is a good thing, but somehow it makes me deeply uncomfortable.'

'You mean because they received the call or because they chose to come?'

'Both,' said Fitzroy. 'I fear what they have up their frilly spinster sleeves. I'm pretty sure the Smiths are actually from Bulgaria. Ruby is from France and Lucy clearly from Italy. I thought we would draw in the Germans too, but I can't pin anyone down.'

'I thought the Grubers were from France.'

'I think so too. Trust the French to have two fingers in the pie.'

'Winifred Mansfield strikes me as formidable.'

Fitzroy nodded. 'She works with Alex. I presume he has told you who he represents?'

'Yes,' I said. 'Are Long and Wools who they appear to be?'

'Army officers with underpants so starched they can barely sit down? No idea. Never heard of them before. Do you think they might be the German representatives? The Germans do have a very odd sense of humour.'

'Speaking of humour: John Groats. John o' Groats?'

'American humour is unsophisticated at best. Watcher rather than helper, I think. Man doesn't drink whisky. Can't trust him.'

'That only leaves Charlie Bingham,' I said.

'Indeed. Again, I have no idea. Which do you want? Charlie or the army pair?'

'I'll take Charlie. Army folks rarely take me seriously.'

'You should be more like Richenda then, and punch them. That would get their attention.'

'I think we have had quite enough violence at this gathering as it is.'

'Yes, what we need is more action!'

'Action?'

Fitzroy coloured faintly. 'You know what I mean, Alice, moving things along.'

I went into luncheon wondering sourly if it had been Ruby or Lucy who had provided the action for Fitzroy last night. However serious the situation he was never a man to pass up an amorous opportunity. And under my roof.

I managed to arrange things so Charlie sat on my left. I had decided that apart from the hosts, no particular arrangement of rank should be upheld. Not least because I didn't know what ranks any of them held. Luncheon was a hot buffet, laid out along one side of the dining room. More elaborate than breakfast, and with many steaming dishes for us to enjoy. There were a quantity of soups and other stews that made me think Mrs Warburton was hoarding her stores in case we were snowed in for longer than we expected. The idea made me shudder. I looked for Hans and Richenda. They did not come in and neither did Bertram. Naturally there was no sign of Esmeralda.

Charlie had got himself a large bowl of oxtail soup and a couple of fresh warm rolls. He broke these into pieces and dropped them into the soup. My surprise must have shown on my face as he gave me a cheeky grin that made him look much younger than I had initially thought. He had one of those faces that might kindly be termed weathered. Fishermen and sailors generally have such a look. His blond hair certainly curled in all directions as if he had been caught in a gale coming into port, and had lost his comb. 'Is it not the thing to drop my bread in my soup?' he said.

'It is your soup and your bread. The choice of what you do with it is entirely your own.'

He frowned slightly. 'Now, is that the politeness of a hostess towards a less-well-brought-up member of the lower classes or some strange metaphor I need to untangle?'

'No metaphor was intended, but I suppose you could imagine I was talking about the choices we make in life. But it would be a bit of a stretch. I'd hope I could come up with a better metaphor, if I was wanting to talk in metaphors.'

'That's rather heavy for a spot of lunchtime chat,' said Charlie, but in a good-humoured tone.

'The world is a serious place,' I said.

'All too so at present,' said Charlie. 'Unlike a lot of them here I've been up to the battle. It's not good.'

'Do you mean we are losing – or are you referring to the loss of life?'

'Madam, I hope you never get to experience such as I saw

during those times. It is as pointless as it is horrendous. That men can bear such things astounds me.'

'This is indeed very serious talk for luncheon,' I said. 'But I fear talk does not stop bullets.'

'No indeed,' said Charlie. 'I am open to suggestions as to what might, but I have yet to hear anyone discuss a workable plan.'

'It seems now we are at war that rumour condenses the clash down to the disagreements between the Kaiser and the King. I have heard it reported that the Kaiser simply thinks he would rule the British Empire in a more accomplished way.'

'But?' said Charlie.

'I suppose he may well think that. But in the years that have led up to the war there have been many moving pieces on the chessboard. It seems to me that the situation is a great deal more complicated than most realise.'

'I heard your husband talking last night. He has an acute political mind.'

I wonder why he does not share such thoughts with his wife, I felt like saying, but instead I said, 'You are the second person to say that to me. Baron von Nacht said similarly.'

'Nacht is an old-style poser. A good man in the field, but hardly a political thinker. He is all derring-do and woo the lady. An outdated creature in the field of espionage.'

Someone, I thought, had better tell Fitzroy this.

'So the modern spy?' I asked.

'Is calmer, cleverer, more circumspect. He waits and watches. They make connections and wait for the time to be right.'

'I assume you talk from experience?'

'Heavens, no,' said Charlie. He gave a short shout of laughter. 'Surely, Mrs Stapleford, you didn't imagine I was a spy?'

By the time luncheon was over I remained baffled as to Charlie's affiliations and with an uncomfortable feeling he was laughing at me. Only very politely, and behind his hand. I said as much to Fitzroy when I caught him after luncheon in the main lobby dressing himself for a walk.

'Jack wants a walk,' he said. 'And I need to clear my head. I had hoped some of these chaps would abandon the games, but I see no such signs. We might as well have set up a room of bridge tables and let them at it.'

'Isn't the snow deeper than Jack?'

'Not everywhere. Besides, he bounces. Don't like that Bingham chap. Eel-like. Talks rubbish.'

'I'm beginning to think you were not that precise when you sent out your call for attendees,' I said.

'That would be von Nacht. Always ready to use a machine-gun when a pistol would do the business just as well. Blunderbuss of a man.'

'I thought he was your friend?'

'He's as much a friend who is not on your side as you can have in this business. So hardly a friend at all.'

'I'm feeling lost,' I admitted.

'As time winds down those who are serious will make clearer their thoughts – or at least I hope so. Come on, Jack. Time to go. Want to come with, Alice?'

'I'm hardly dressed for it.'

Fitzroy looked me up and down as if realising for the first time I was wearing a morning dress. 'Quite right,' he said. 'I much prefer you in trousers.'

I felt myself flush red. 'Good . . .'

'You're much more agile then,' he said and walked out of the door before I could protest.

I heard hurried steps behind me, and turned to see my husband fast approaching. 'That old Fitzroy heading off?'

'Walking the dog,' I said. 'Do you think it reasonable women should be so confined by their clothes?'

Bertram blinked. 'Not top of my list for consideration at present. Stays too tight after luncheon? Speaking of which, is there any left for yours truly or did the guests polish it off.'

'Mrs Warburton will be able to sort you out in the kitchen,' I said.

'Excellent,' said Bertram, brightening considerably. 'I shall head there at once.' He jerked his head back towards the stairs. 'Half of them are going off for a nap now they've stuffed themselves at our table.' He leaned over and gave me a peck on the cheek. 'You look ravishing even if you have overeaten. Meet up over the tea things?'

I nodded.

'Oh, I said you'd look in on Hans. You don't mind, do you? Can't be seen to talk to the opposition!'

Chapter Twelve

The Scorned

I ended up having to ask my housekeeper as to the whereabouts of my sister-in-law. Mrs T reported that she had been given the small tower room. We didn't exactly have towers at White Orchards. The building was a hodge-podge of styles and attempts at reconstruction. One corner had for no apparent reason an upper level, and Bertram had taken to calling it the small tower, rather than the more apt description, 'that odd bit that juts up'.

But as I made my way up the staircase I could see why Richenda might have chosen this. The staircase was tight. My dress scraped the sides of the wall, and I wear the smoothest-contoured clothes decency will allow. I found the limewashed walls overbearing and confining. I now automatically looked for the exits in every space I entered, and this section of the house was a dead end. However, for someone like Richenda I suppose the close confines could suggest safety. Rather like her being a bear in a den.

I knocked on the homely wooden door. A moment later the door opened an inch and I saw her face. If there was disappointment written on it, it was gone in a second. She opened the door and ushered me in.

Mrs T had made the room as comfortable as possible with bright linens (Richenda was a lover of bright and frequently clashing colours). The sash window was open a few inches, and I hurried across to one of the two chairs by the hearth that had a roaring fire. Richenda lingered by the window.

'How are you now?' I asked.

Richenda sniffed. 'I've always known, you know.'

'I wondered if you suspected.'

'Did you know?'

I shook my head. 'I suspected, but I never had any proof. But then I thought perhaps you had an agreement.'

'Most men have mistresses,' said Richenda, raising her chin defiantly. 'My father did.'

'It's not uncommon. Will you not come and sit by the fire? You'll catch your death by that window.'

'I don't care,' she said, and gave a sudden sob.

'Yes, you do,' I said firmly. 'You have the children. Besides, you have walked in on something that involves the lives of countless people. You are deeply hurt by Hans. I understand that. But I am afraid there is always a bigger picture.' It sounded unkind, even to my own ears.

'Then why did you insist I came?' asked Richenda.

I fairly gaped at her. After a moment I managed to collect myself enough to say, 'Do you have the letter?'

Richenda gave me a puzzled look, but at least she was no longer on the verge of crying. She opened the top drawer of the dresser and handed me a piece of paper. 'It's more a note than a letter.'

Richenda, you must come at once. Hans is here and he needs you. Euphemia

It looked remarkably like my hand, although not at all my style. But in such a direct appeal I doubted Richenda would have considered that.

'When did you receive this?'

'Yesterday. I caught a train to the nearest station and got a drayman to bring me. It cost me every penny I had on me.'

'I didn't write this, Richenda. I didn't even know Esmeralda would be coming here. May I keep this?'

Richenda finally sat down at the hearth. 'That's rather intriguing. Why would anyone want me to come to one of your funny meetings?'

I couldn't help but smile at this. Richenda had suspicions about my work for the Crown, and she had always been keen on sniffing out a mystery.

'Do you remember that time we searched Hans's attic for a mad wife?' she said suddenly.

'I do. We were quite the adventurers.'

'And that suffragette march?'

'I hit a policeman with a shoe. I ended up in jail. I don't think I ever told Bertram about that.'

Richenda gave a weak smile. 'I wondered if that's why Hans is having affairs.'

'Looking for excitement, you mean?'

'But I'm left at home. The most excitement I get is wondering where he is.' Richenda gave a bitter laugh.

I took a deep breath. 'I think you need to decide what you want to do next.'

'You don't mean divorce! I couldn't stand the scandal.'

'No, I didn't think you would want to go through that. But you could lead separate lives. I think you should make the decision – whether you forgive him or not.'

'Take control?'

'Be proud of the white, purple and green.'

I left her then, feeling as if I had done my bit for moral support. I couldn't imagine what more I could say to Hans. He knew I had disapproved of his antics and now he had been caught out. He had to pay the price. On the other hand, I was a little concerned about what Esmeralda might be up to. Mrs T had sent up a luncheon on a tray, but I doubted she would stay sequestered in her room.

As I went downstairs I noticed the house was quiet. There is something about a blanket of snow that sets one thinking of hibernation and gathering in the folds. It's a primitive response to the season. A desire to protect and survive until the summer and the warmth of the sun returns. It could be a peaceful time. But it was also a time of death for those too frail or ill to make it through the winter. Maybe the peace within these walls would remind our guests of the young men, hardly more than boys, dying in the cold trenches, and how peace was needed across the world. For the first time this year I felt a small stir of excitement about Christmas. If Richenda forgave Hans perhaps they too could join Bertram and me, and Fitzroy. Fitzroy seemed to have become as permanent a Christmas fixture as the Christmas Eve tree.

I heard a crash below. I hurried downstairs immediately, and found a snowman standing in a mess of fallen canes and umbrellas. Jack was jumping up and down and whiffling. 'The dog did it,' said Fitzroy.

'Of course, and nothing to do with the fact you look like more ice than man. You must be frozen. Get rid of that cape and come in to the fire. I have something to tell you.'

'Will I like it?'

'Probably not.'

'Then I insist on a glass of hot toddy and a bone for Jack.'

In the small library, seated in front of the fire, I showed him Richenda's letter. Jack was curled at our feet with a pork bone and making happy little growls as he chewed it. Fitzroy took the letter with one hand, and as he read the contents he finished the toddy in one long gulp. Then swore viciously.

'As bad as that?' I asked.

'It seems that the call that Alex and I put out was not as precise as I had hoped.'

'I thought you invited people individually?'

'Don't be naïve, Alice, it was all done through the usual smoke and mirrors.'

'But you said people gave their word . . .'

'Their word to behave was implicit in their agreed attendance.'

'If that is the case, we cannot presume that all the people present are here to find a solution to the war.'

'No, we can't.' He swore again, this time adding some idioms that I had not heard before.

'I hope you can be as creative in untangling this mess we're in,' I said.

'So do I. For all I know we have hostile assassins here.'

I put my head in my hands. 'Please don't tell Bertram that.'

'He will need to be on his guard!' said Fitzroy, pulling the bell. 'I need another one of these.' He held up the glass. 'Do you want one too?'

'No,' I said. 'I just want all these people out of my home.'

Chapter Thirteen

Perspectives

Fitzroy and I parted somewhat coolly. He was away to confer with Alex about what could have gone wrong in the communication channels they used. I floated around, ensuring the guests had all they needed, and encouraging small groups to confer. Or at least that's what I hoped it looked like I was doing. In reality I was both keeping watch and attempting to identify those who might prove a threat.

You can tell a lot about a person from the way they hold themselves. Privilege will always out in the tilt of the head, the length of the stride (in a man) and way he sets his shoulders. But when someone is trained, as I had been, you also notice how they move. How they shift their weight from foot to foot. Whether they are light enough, or agile enough, to dodge an incoming blow. Whether their eyes seek not only exits when they enter a room, but reflections in which to watch their back. On more than one occasion I have rooted out an enemy spy by their movements. But every damn person here, with the exception of Hans, Esmeralda and Richenda, was a trained operative. Seeking clues as to their intentions would be a struggle.

I was thinking about how only two young hot-headed males could have been as brash as to start this endeavour when I rounded a corner and almost walked straight into Esmeralda. She sprang back lithe as a cat. I half expected her to hiss at me. 'What are you doing down here?' I demanded.

'What? Did you expect me to stay in my room? I am as wronged as anyone here.' This was a different Esmeralda from the one I had known in Scotland. There was fire in her eyes.

I squared up to her as I would with any person at the beginning of a fight. I had no intention of striking her, but I wanted to send a message that had strength beyond words. 'You came to my house under false pretences. Hans had no right to invite you.'

'He did that in your presence, and you did not complain.'

'I did not take him seriously,' I said. I knew it was a weak reply. At the time I had been on the track of a killer, and I had not wanted to spare the time to deal with Hans and his attempt at seduction. I had told myself the couple were as bad as each other, but my conscience had pricked me. I had never got to the bottom of who Esmeralda was, and why she followed us so eagerly to Edinburgh. 'You are the mistress of a married man, and you have committed adultery in my home, when you were expressly given a room far away from him.'

As if she had transformed into shattering glass, Esmeralda folded over clutching her stomach, her face a picture of despair. I took a step towards her, and heard her say softly, 'So it was his wife.'

I approached closely and laid a hand on her shoulder. 'Let us go into a place more private than this corridor.' She allowed me to lead her to the smoking room. At this time of day it would not be in use, and so I hoped we would encounter no one other. The air in the room was so cold we saw our breath in front of us, curling like smoke from invisible pipes. I sat her down in Bertram's favourite chair. The wingback shielded one from most of the draughts in the room, and it hid her from sight should anyone come to the door.

I gathered two of the throws from a settee. I passed one to her, placed the other around my shoulders and brought over a footstool to sit upon. The temperature of the room had given her alabaster skin a faintly blueish tinge, and she huddled down under the throw. She looked about her with some curiosity. Her gaze rested on the large humidor on a small black lacquer table.

'A present for my husband's last birthday,' I said, relieved she had not broken down into tears. 'This room is largely my husband's domain. It is rarely in use during the day. I apologise for the cold.'

'Yes,' she said in a dead voice, 'the weather is most unexpected.' Her gaze was distant, as if she was looking at something far beyond me. 'I imagine you get ghosts here. People drown in the Fens, don't they?'

'It has been known to happen. The snow does not usually fall so thickly at this time of year,' I said, redirecting her morbid thoughts. I was watching her closely. Had the cold calmed her distress or was she sinking into some kind of placid hysteria? Was she thinking of throwing herself into the Fens?

Suddenly, her eyes snapped into focus. 'I did not know he was married until you told me when I arrived here.'

I raised an eyebrow. 'Even if that is true, you did not behave like a lady.'

For a second I thought she was about to laugh, but her tone, when it came, was thin and bitter with ire. 'Ha! I was indiscreet. I admit that. But those of your class are hardly paragons.'

'Perhaps not,' I said. 'But I keep a Christian household.' It sounded prim even unto my own ears. It was a long time since I had been a regular church attendant. I also kept a Fitzroy in my house, and I knew full well the extent of his immorality.

'I wonder if it is because I am a woman that you disrespect me?' she said, picking at the edge of the cover that hung about her shoulders and hitting the mark with more accuracy than I liked. 'It is certainly because I am a woman that I am in this position. But then you have never liked me, have you, Euphemia?'

'I only know you by your actions.'

'Then allow me the privilege of putting these into context for you.' Before I could answer she continued on, and while her voice remained low, it cut the air between us with its cold anger. 'As I told you, my husband died in your war. We had married young and had little between us. He was set on a good career, and I believe things would have gone well for us. Then came the war, and he was killed. He drowned.' She paused. I was torn between appreciating how she underplayed her story, to pitiful effect, and an increasing concern that she might be telling the truth.

'He had made a will leaving what little we had to his brother.'

'Why would he do such a thing?'

'His family is most old-fashioned. They believe the female sex should not be burdened with money.' She lowered her head for a second. 'I would have been most content to be a wife and mother.' She paused. 'I think my husband believed his brother would care for me, but he too was caught up in the war. Besides, I do not think he liked me much. He did secure for me a place to stay with an elderly aunt. I was to be a housekeeper-cum-companion. As he told me to my face, I was penniless and I would have to earn my keep somehow.'

'That was cruel,' I said.

'He did not approve of our marriage, and he was most concerned about money. The aunt lived secluded, too old and infirm to go into society; she would be grateful for my companionship. I am sure even you, with your fine house and clever husband, can see this future held no appeal for me. So when I met Hans, or Frederick, as he called himself then, and he was interested in me, I thought I had found my salvation.'

'You thought he meant marriage? On such a short acquaintance? You cannot expect me to believe that.'

She hung her head. 'I admit I thought that marriage might not immediately be on his mind. He was clearly a man of the world, and I was a widow. I understood things in a way an unmarried woman would not.'

'You thought to entrap him?'

'No. Yes. That is a harsh term. I thought we liked one another, and that if I allowed him to be carried away by his passion, he would eventually marry me because he was a gentleman. I rather counted on you to make him do the right thing. I thought you were his cousin at the time.'

'I am his sister-in-law.'

Esmeralda frowned. Her voice and her expression changed to

reflect genuine confusion. 'You saw the way things were going between us. You might even have guessed my intentions, why did you not warn me? Hans said you are a suffragette. You know how this world is ruled by men. Why did you not, as woman to woman, warn me that he was married?'

I got up and pulled the cover more closely around me. 'It is too cold to continue this discussion. As you see we are all trapped by the weather. I suggest for your own sake you keep to your room until there is a plan for how to proceed. I would not lock you in your chamber, nor forbid you from wandering about the house, but I genuinely believe you would be better away from Hans and his wife. Whatever he may have told you, Hans will not leave his wife. Theirs is a marriage of convenience.'

'You mean she is rich?'

'There are children,' I said, and I thought I saw real pain in her eyes.

'I see. I shall return to my room and remain there till the weather clears.'

'Ask my servants for anything you need.'

'I am grateful for your hospitality,' she said. 'This is not how I wished things to be.'

I let her leave first. I stood in the empty room shivering and searching my conscience. I had thought her the adventuress. She had told me something of her story before, but I had not seen her as a victim. Instead, I had seen it as Hans causing problems. Hans had more than once propositioned me, and I had come to think of his flirtatious nature as an irritant. But then I had a home, a husband and my own income. I was in a very different place to Esmeralda. I might tell myself I had been focusing on my mission, but the truth was I had never considered her as a person. She had merely been an annoyance. And yet, something bothered me. I had that uncomfortable feeling you get when someone tells you a half-truth. Could there be another reason why her brother-in-law wanted her hidden away? Was this not the first time she had tried entrapment?

Chapter Fourteen

Parlour Games

'Whole bally thing sounds like some maudlin Irish song,' said Fitzroy when I relayed the conversation to him later that day. We were snatching a quick drink before dinner in the library. Any moment I expected Bertram to join us, so we could lay out our plans for this evening. 'You think she is telling the truth?'

'Some of it at least. I do believe she is – lost.'

Fitzroy frowned. 'It's not like you to not recognise the plight of another.'

'No,' I said, looking down at my feet. 'I think I may have behaved rather inconsiderately.' I looked up. 'But I was terribly worried about you at the front. And saving Griffin.'

'I wonder if he would . . . thing is, we will have to do something with the girl. Even I wouldn't turn a girl out of the house without a penny to her name. Wouldn't even do that to a dog.'

I smiled. 'First, you like dogs more than most people, and second, dogs don't use money.'

Fitzroy's lips quirked at the corners. 'Too true. The thing is, Euphemia, even if the woman is an adventuress, as you so quaintly put it, that doesn't mean she isn't in a damn awful position.'

'Are you offering to take Hans's place?' I said as lightly as I could.

'No, thank you. Leaving aside the fact that she is seeking safe harbour in matrimony, and I'm doing my damn best to keep myself out of that particular port, I don't trust her as far as I could throw her.'

'So you think...'

'I don't think anything. She just gives me the willies. Can't explain it. Might be the matrimonial emanations. Still doesn't mean we can leave her to starve.'

I sighed. 'At least she's not a spy.'

'Yes, thank goodness. We have enough of those.'

'Did you have any luck with Alex, figuring out what happened with your message.'

'No. Did you have any luck figuring out Charlie Bingham?'

'No.'

'Lord, what a pair we are!' said Fitzroy. 'The King's finest!'

The door opened and Bertram came in. 'Oh, jolly good! You're on the whisky already.' He sidled up to the fire, pausing only to give me a quick peck on the cheek. 'Goodness knows it's cold. We'll have burned down the whole damn woods the rate we're stoking the fires. And still parts of the house feel as cold as a tomb!'

'Don't,' I said. 'I've already had people asking me if there are ghosts walking nearby.'

Fitzroy raised an eyebrow.

'Drowned in the Fens,' I said.

'I doubt there is a foot of land that someone has not died on before,' said Bertram, helping himself to a large measure of whisky. 'Human beings have been around rather a long time, and during that time they have only ever had their small allotment of years.'

'That is profound,' I said to Bertram. 'And before dinner. Are you faring well, my love?'

'It's a fairly obvious observation,' said Fitzroy, 'but I agree your husband is normally at his cheeriest before dinner. What has happened?'

'Apart from the breaking apart of my sister's marriage?'

'That was always on the cards,' said Fitzroy.

'Yes,' said Bertram. He took a strong swig and shook his head like a dog drying its ears. 'But not here in my home. Besides, that's not it. Your people give me the creeps. To play the game, that's what you call it, isn't it? When so many lives are at stake. I see nothing good coming from this gathering, and I don't trust those phony English blighters, the colonel and his subordinate, further than I could spit them! I think they're Germans.'

'That would be good,' said Fitzroy. 'It would mean they are taking this effort seriously. To end the war, I mean.'

Bertram shook his head. 'No, they never contribute. They only sneak up behind others and listen. Very stealthy they are too. On more than one occasion I've had cause to start. Even dropped a scone once. One of our cook's best, warm from the oven.' He frowned ferociously. 'Definitely not cricket. And the Colonel and the Lieutenant know Esmeralda too. Found them all chatting in the morning room. Thick as thieves.'

'What were they talking about?' I said quickly.

'Hiring staff,' said Bertram. 'The difficulty of such things. I think the older one has an eye on our cook.'

Fitzroy snorted in a disdaining manner and poured himself another glass. 'I think if we want to move things along we should suggest a parlour game after dinner. Time to get them to loosen up a bit, let down some of the barriers, familiarise themselves with foreign territory, as it were.'

'As you and Lucy did last night? Or was it Ruby?' asked Bertram.

Fitzroy downed the rest of his glass in one and set it down on the sideboard with an alarmingly loud chink. 'I will be talking discreetly to everyone here. Von Nacht and I have the advantage of being known even if we do not yet know who all the parties represent.' Then he turned on his heel and stalked out before either of us could speak.

'Looks like I've upset him,' said Bertram with a slight smile. 'Best aperitif for dinner!' And he rubbed his hands together like a naughty schoolboy who has got one over on his headmaster.

'We are trying to achieve a serious outcome,' I said gently.

'Dearest wife, this was always a long shot of a plan and it is failing.'

'But you agreed to it.'

'Oh, my mission is accomplished. Our cellar is well stocked for

Christmas. The drive is re-gravelled and the stables fitted out as servants' quarters. None of this, not to mention a few other trifles, has been done at our expense. Plus, Fitzroy also owes me a large favour.' He set down his own glass much more carefully. 'That it is also turning out to be a distressing flop for our spymaster is the icing on the cake. I shall see you at dinner.'

'And you accuse us of playing games,' I said. But he pretended not to hear me. I set down my half-drunk glass. I had no appetite for it. Whisky, I generally associate with the calm and restful time after a day well spent. As a stiffener for the event ahead, it was doing nothing but making me faintly nauseous. I could see why Fitzroy had suggested the cover of an English country-house game. I picked up the glass and tossed off the last of it, hoping to find some courage in the bottom. I did not. I sighed and made my way towards the dining room.

Dinner was again superb and applauded by all the diners. For such a mix of foreign palates this was a remarkable feat by our cook. Perhaps Bertram was right and I should be watching for any approaches to poach her. I must see her this evening, praise her and offer her a rise. To have such a treasure in the Fens was truly remarkable.

As the diners were scraping up the last of their lemon mousse, Fitzroy tapped his spoon against his glass and stood up. 'Ladies and gentlemen, I hope you will agree that we owe a toast to our hosts and to the splendid hospitality they have shown us. To Mr and Mrs Stapleford!'

The toast was warmly echoed. I looked around the table and saw happy indolence on the faces surrounding me. Perhaps we would have had better results if we had kept them hungry. Our guests looked far too fat and pleased with themselves.

'I have another toast and a suggestion to make. Despite my best efforts, I fear we have all remained strangers to one another, so I suggest a loosening of the stays after our repast by the playing of a traditional country-house game.' Fitzroy surveyed those around the table. There was nothing but mild interest on the faces of our guests.

'The game is called Sardines and refers to the close proximity that these tiny fish have once stacked into their tin. We here represent many of the nations of the advanced world, and all of us find ourselves pressured into a war that is becoming a war of attrition where it is no longer a question of who will win, but how much we will each lose. We have an opportunity—' He broke off. 'But enough of such analogies. The game is simply that one person hides in this house, and the others have to find him or her. When you find the first hidden person then you must join them. The game ends when there is only one person left alone. Bertram, as our host, will be our adjudicator and remain outside the game. He will call time when all but the last person is in the tin, as it were. You may hunt in groups or alone. It is a surprisingly enjoyable game. The only other rule I suggest is that no physical violence may be employed.' He gave a smirk at this. 'This is not a usual rule, but we are all individuals used to working in the shadows. Perhaps in this game we will unlock similarities in the dark.'

To my enormous surprise the idea of the game went down well. Some numbered balls were placed in a sack. Fitzroy, choosing number one, was to be the first to hide. The rest of us picked a number that would decide the order in which we left the dining room. Fitzroy was allowed five minutes to hide, and then the rest of us would leave the dining room at two-minute intervals. Fitzroy handed Bertram a stopwatch. I intervened at this moment to beg for fifteen minutes' leeway to allow a powder-room break for the ladies and time for the servants to clear the table and remove its leaves. We could then return to the room refreshed and begin the game – and with sufficient space!

The truth was I did not fancy playing Sardines with any of the people here. I wasn't in the least bit sure that I wouldn't end up with, if not a weapon, a wandering hand in a soft part of my anatomy. I would prefer to confront a fighting opponent. Navigating the politics of a tipsy guest whose proclivities were straying over the acceptable line was a situation that I disliked far more. Especially if I was bound to eschew a violent response.

In the end I did not make it back to the dining room for my turn. I was taken away to deal with a crisis that had befallen my dear friend Merry. I had known Merry since my first days of working as a servant. Her husband was missing in the war. In the interim, it transpired she had become close to our local doctor. The arrival of a letter saying her husband had been traced alive in a POW camp, and the confirmation of a blossoming seed of Merry's relationship with our doctor, had occurred that very day. Merry, in great distress, came to me for help. I will go into no more details other than to say she spent an hour crying on my shoulder, while I tried and failed to find a happy solution to her predicament. I agreed to help in any way I could, and eventually she returned the short distance to her home with the promise that we would speak again tomorrow.

Wrung out by this crisis, I found myself overwhelmed with emotion. I had myself miscarried a child a few short months ago. Only Fitzroy and his man, Griffin, knew this as it had happened during a mission. I had chosen, against Fitzroy's strong advice, not to inform Bertram that I had lost his child by continuing to work on a difficult mission when I – and only I – knew I was pregnant.

The thought of joining in the damned game was too much for me. It now struck me as obscene that we could not all sit down at a table and openly discuss the war and what it was costing us. We were all motivated to come up with a solution. It struck me that in truth spies spend much of their time believing they are more potent than they are. Yes, we might be the recipients of delicate and dangerous secrets, but the reality was we had little sway over the cumulative actions of our masters. This whole house party was, in short, pure nonsense.

I was in control of myself enough that I knew I needed a few moments alone before I greeted the other guests once more. If it was possible I should also avoid Fitzroy. I had had quite enough of him and his ideas.

Without conscious thought I made my way to the small library off the library proper. It had always been my haven in the evenings. I passed Bertram patrolling the halls.

'He was right,' he said to me. 'The bally lot are running around and having a good time. I swear even those two old Russian ladies cracked a smile. I heard a cackle too. I pity any man who gets cornered in a dark place by them.'

'I take it no one is playing the game properly,' I said.

'That's generally the point of Sardines,' said my husband. 'People getting together in the dark and, well, I suppose behaving badly.'

'I should have known it would be Fitzroy's favourite game.'

'Hold hard, my darling. Your spies aren't up to that sort of naughtiness. They've been laughing, yes, but I'm hearing discussions rather than maidenly shrieks. Not that I think Mimi or Gertrude would tempt anyone to do . . .'

'Lucy and Ruby.'

'Oh yes,' agreed my husband eagerly. 'Lovely ladies, but very professional I found. Ruby has some truly interesting ideas about how Italy's geographical position in the world makes it feel all liaisons are fragile.'

'Because it's in the middle,' I said crushingly.

'It's more than that. Their people differ so much from north to south – again, more geographical stuff. They also have the big vein of mountains down the middle.'

'Have they found Fitzroy yet?'

'Three of them have. Are you going to have a try?'

I shook my head. My husband looked at me in genuine concern. 'Has something happened?'

'Other than the obvious?' I saw the hurt expression in his eyes. 'I'm sorry, Bertram. I have no issue with you. I feel this whole meeting has been a bad idea. And . . .'

'I do believe it was worth trying,' said Bertram. 'The stakes . . .' He trailed off. 'What else?'

'Merry has got herself into difficulties. I don't know how to help her.'

'That doctor? I thought she was running close to the wind.'

'I didn't notice. I might have been able to . . .'

'Merry is a love, but she has always been flighty. Don't blame yourself. Will he not marry her? I'll have a word if you wish.'

'Her husband has been located in a POW camp.'

'Dammit,' said Bertram. 'That is a problem. I'm sure we can sort something out.'

I felt tears pricking my eyes. 'But I do not believe she will be able to keep her baby.'

Bertram shook his head. 'No, I suspect not.'

I felt tears trickling down my face. 'The loss of—' I broke off on a sob.

Bertram reached out his arms to me, but I ran away, my hand over my face. He called after me. I managed to say something like, 'I cannot . . .' and left him in the hallway. I knew he would worry, but he would also feel he had to stay there for our guests and Fitzroy's stupid game.

I fled into the library and threw myself down into a seat by the fire, and sobbed my heart out. All I could think about was the child I had lost. Merry, even if the pregnancy went full term, would know that pain. The best solution would be for a member of her family to take in the child. I knew she had sisters. But she would never be able to own the child while her husband lived, and even then I suspected she would not want to mar their life with the stigma of a baby born out of wedlock.

I recognised I was overwrought. I thought I was past this. Would these feelings haunt me for the rest of my life? When it had happened Fitzroy had been my staunchest ally. I had seen the side of him that showed how much he cared for me. A side he usually did his best to hide. But now I still carried my pain, and he was off chasing lovely foreign spies. And I feared should I ever tell Bertram, who has always disliked my spying, he would never forgive me if I told him I had risked and lost our pregnancy. My husband trusted me more than any husband has ever trusted a wife, and how had I repaid him? I had formed a strong affection for another man – an unworthy man – and I had killed our child.

I do not know how long I cried, but eventually I ran out of tears. I felt exhausted. I sat quietly, staring at the fire. It was then I became aware of voices coming from the main library. It was Fitzroy and Esmeralda. I pricked up my ears.

Chapter Fifteen

I Argue with Fitzroy

'So you have crept out from your hidey-hole?' said Esmeralda.

'Oh hello,' said Fitzroy. 'Not exactly. Needed a little something. I didn't know you were playing?' His voice was friendly, but wary.

'I'm not, but you cannot expect me to stay locked in my room!'

'I would have thought your common sense would tell you to stay away from the party. Whether you knew Hans was married or not, you are marked as a loose woman. I do not vouch for any of the men here.'

'Does that include yourself?'

Fitzroy gave a bark of laughter. 'Especially myself, madam.'

I heard the sound of her dress rustling. 'I think you and I could come to an arrangement.'

'I think not,' said Fitzroy.

'You don't know what you are refusing. We need to talk privately.'

'I must get back to the game.'

'You should know I am well versed in the game. I am very good. You should try me. Our ideas may well align.'

'Tempting,' said Fitzroy in a voice that had descended to a low purr. 'But I must, at least, defer.'

'I shall find you.'

'You can try, madam. But I am not that easy to catch,' said Fitzroy. I heard the sound of his running footsteps, and then a delighted laugh of Esmeralda's, and the swish of her skirts as she pursued him.

I knew the extent of Fitzroy's faults more than anyone else. Usually, I overlooked them. Usually, they were not on such rampant display before me. When I thought of good and worthy Bertram, who would walk through hellfire for me, and whose trust I had so abused for the sake of adventuring with Fitzroy, I felt sick to my stomach.

I stayed in my seat sinking deeper into despair. Men such as Fitzroy, the impetuous, the rash, the adventurous, were the root of all evil in the world. It was men with such qualities that kept the war going. I was most certainly not in the mood for company when the door flew open and Fitzroy appeared.

He closed the door in a flash with careful quietness. Then signalled to me to be quiet. His colour was up, and his hair dishevelled, but a smile lingered on his lips. Whatever he was doing he was clearly enjoying himself. Footsteps ran past the door. Fitzroy turned the key in the lock, which we hardly ever used, and came over to help himself to a glass of whisky.

'I think it's all going swimmingly,' he said as he chinked the decanter against the glass in a way I especially hated. 'Want another?'

'No,' I said softly.

He turned, holding up his drink and smiling. His expression faded when he saw my face. He set his drink back down on the tray and pulled up the other seat. 'My dear girl, what has happened?' His voice changed to a sharper tone. 'Has anyone harmed you? Has that wretched husband of yours done something to distress you?'

'Bertram is a far better man than you will ever be.'

Both Fitzroy's eyebrows rose, but he kept his tone calm. He reached over and took the glass again. 'I do not believe that was ever in doubt,' he said.

'You talked him into this ridiculous spectacular,' I said. 'He believed you were doing it for the sake of King and Country.'

'I am,' said Fitzroy, sitting back in his seat. 'You know that is the basis of everything I do.'

'Oh yes,' I said, feeling my temper rise. 'And Ruby and Lucy and even Esmeralda. What you do with them is for the sake of the nation, isn't it? Your lust has nothing to do with it.'

'Euphemia, don't be crude. It doesn't suit you.'

'And under my roof. You have made my home a den of lechery and vice.'

Fitzroy took a sip. 'I think you might have had one too many of these, old girl. I know what happened with Richenda and Hans is distressing, but in the big picture it's not significant.'

'At least Hans is open about what he is!'

'I don't believe Esmeralda would agree with you on that point.' The spymaster crossed his legs and tilted his head. 'Have you been crying?'

'Why would you care?' I snapped.

Fitzroy blinked at me. A curious expression went across his face, something halfway between confusion and concern. 'I think you should tell me what has been going on.'

I stood up and began to pace. 'Oh, don't worry, it's nothing that will affect your grand plan. Just another life ruined.'

'Anyone I know?' I could hear his attempt at a light-hearted tone.

I turned on him. 'Anyone you know? Anyone you know? You don't care the snap of your fingers for any of us, and I'm beginning to think you view espionage as only a game.'

'Well, actually, historically,' began Fitzroy in the sort of voice he uses when he's teaching me something, 'we do refer to it as the Great Game.'

'Oh, shut up!'

'Alice! You have no business to talk to me like that.'

'You only play the commanding officer card when you're losing,' I said, even though I knew that was unfair. 'Look what your hubris has done! You've brought some of the most dangerous people in the world together without sanction. Did you explain to Bertram you were asking him to commit treason?'

'I haven't done anything of the kind,' said Fitzroy, rising to his feet. 'This isn't like you, Alice. If you tell me what's happened, I will do anything in my power to help you. You know that.'

'I'm phoning Morley in the morning,' I said. 'He needs to know about this whole charade before things get further out of hand.'

The colour drained from Fitzroy's face. 'To what end?' he said slowly. 'To see me hanged for treason or only to damage my career irreparably? The one thing I live to do.'

'Ha!' I said. 'You know damn well you'll get nothing but a rap on the knuckles. You always land on your feet, like a wretched cat. But this time you have gone too far. You need to be stopped. Discussing with a foreign agent the kidnap of our sovereign!'

'If you tell him that he will have me shot.'

'Then why did you do it? Why should I have to cover for you, and put myself and my family in danger?'

Fitzroy had put down his drink and was now standing very still. 'I have always had your back,' he said. 'I have always kept your secrets. I have always supported you.'

This was, of course, completely true, and so it only infuriated me further. 'It was you who drew me into this. You've admitted that since your failure to save my father, you've watched me and pulled me into your sordid little world.'

For a moment I saw his face fold in upon itself as if in great pain, but the next his expression was blank and genial. 'You must do as you wish,' he said, stepping towards the door. 'As to what you do tomorrow, whether you contact Morley or not is entirely a matter for your own conscience. I have nothing further to add.'

I threw my glass at the closing door. It missed him and, hitting the edge, shattered into myriad pieces. The falling shards caught the light of the fire and it looked for a short time as if I had set the world alight.

Chapter Sixteen

From Frying Pan to Fire

I spent a bad night, tossing and turning to such an extent that Bertram went to sleep in his dressing room. In his case, it wasn't so much a conscious choice as more a muttering and grumbling as he slumped his way to the cot bed, trailing a blanket behind him like a sleepy bear. I had the impression he might be quite surprised when he woke up there in the morning. On any other occasion I would have found this episode of my husband's somnambulance amusing.

I felt utterly dreadful, and it wasn't due to the whisky. Although my stomach felt sour and my head ached.

I genuinely felt that Fitzroy had strong-armed us into a difficult situation, but I knew full well that under his bravado he genuinely despaired at the loss of life occurring in the war. It made him sick to his soul. I still felt his response in talking Bertram into this event, before I could question his intentions, was foolish and ill thought out. But I recognised it for what it was, the desperate act of a man who wanted to see the slaughter stop. He had been up to the front on more than one occasion, and it had affected him deeply. He had always been the kind of man who hated taking a life in the course of his duty and always tried to find another way. In the end he did what was necessary, but it marked him in a way that, oddly, it did not mark me. I knew myself for a pragmatist – when I was not overindulging in my emotions! Whereas though he would never admit it, Fitzroy was, at heart, a romantic.

In all our time together, he had never turned his back on me.

Whatever we encountered, he had – annoyingly – stood by my side. Annoyingly, because he had gentlemanly concerns over me that he seemed to have over no other woman. He told me again and again in training how he wanted me to be his equal in the field. And yet, every time there was danger, he did his best to stand between it and me. Fitzroy might have multiple liaisons with various ladies, but I knew he loved none of them. There might be friendship between them, even fleeting affection, but nothing stronger, and I also knew he took pains to make this clear to his paramours. He made no false promises. Though he would never say it to me, I knew he cared for, valued, maybe even loved (in a platonic sense) only one woman: me.

Instead of reasoning with him when I saw how things were going, I had threatened to betray him. To turn him into our superior officer. If I had stabbed him through the heart I couldn't have hurt him more.

I didn't sleep a wink.

I rehearsed several times over how I would apologise at breakfast. How I could repair the damage to our relationship and still make him see that we needed to draw this event to an end. Perhaps it could have gone differently, but I saw only danger, not redemption. Above all, I had to tell him again and again until he believed it that I would never betray him. I had spoken in anger, while dealing with the greatest wound I have ever been asked to bear – the loss of my pregnancy – now redoubled when I must help my dearest friend give up her child.

By the time the morning came my headache had become so bad, it felt like I was screaming inside my own head.

The bedroom door opened. 'I say, Euphemia, you awake? Only there's someone screaming downstairs,' said Bertram.

I sat up in bed, holding a hand to my forehead. 'Is there?' I said. 'I thought it—'

An ear-splitting scream rent the air.

'Good God,' I said, slipping out of bed and pulling on a gown. 'That sounds serious.'

'Probably Richenda having a go at Hans,' said Bertram. 'Could I ask you . . .'

'It's fine. I'm going,' I said as I tied the belt of my gown.

'You look bloody awful,' said Bertram, concern in his voice.

I gave him a peck on the cheek. 'I'll send a servant if I need your help.'

I slipped past him and ran lightly down the stairs. I still felt terrible, but my training had kicked in. Sometimes you just had to get on and deal with things. Another scream. It did not sound like Richenda, and it was coming from downstairs. This time no other doors had burst open. The spies were either too overcome from last night's shenanigans or were not to be tempted out again for another cry of wolf.

Only this time, it was different. I rounded the top of the stairs to see Esmeralda lying on her side with her lifeblood flowing from her, while Richenda stood over her, a bloody knife in her hand.

Chapter Seventeen

Did She Do It?

'I didn't do it!'

I froze for a moment then I ran down the stairs, lifting my nightdress high above my ankles without thought. I knelt down by Esmeralda. Her eyelids fluttered. I put pressure against the wound in her side, but the blood flowed between my fingers.

'I didn't do it!' said Richenda again.

'Help!' I shouted. 'We need help!' I heard doors opening upstairs and the sound of running feet.

I leaned harder on her side. It is always shocking how warm blood is. 'Stay with us, Esmeralda,' I said. 'Help is coming.'

Her face was chalk-white. She looked up at me. I saw a gleam of recognition, but then her eyes began to lose focus. 'Stay with us.'

Von Nacht arrived in his dressing gown and embroidered slippers. You notice the strangest things when people are dying. 'A doctor?' he asked.

'In the village. The servants know where to find him. No, wait. Send for Griffin.'

'I will send for both. But the weather is bad.' Willoughby was running towards us, and von Nacht issued instructions to him before returning to my side.

'Let me see,' he said.

'I daren't let off the pressure.'

'I will find something to bind it.'

'Napkins, in the dining room.'

'I didn't do it,' Richenda said once more. Von Nacht looked

round as if noticing her for the first time. He relieved her of the knife but then ran off in search of napkins. Esmeralda's eyelids fluttered again.

'The doctor is on his way. All will be well,' I said, but she turned her head away.

Von Nacht returned within moments. He competently folded some napkins into a pad, and then with a belt he bound it around her body. He had to move her slightly to do this, and she groaned. Another gush of blood followed. Von Nacht caught my eye, and he gave a tiny shake of his head.

I leaned down close to her head. 'Esmeralda, who did this to you?'

Her eyes refocused. Each word was formed slowly but clearly as if with great effort. 'It was a good game,' she said. Her voice grew quieter and I had to lean closer to hear. I still could not make it all out. 'Lost . . . Hans . . . sorry . . . peace.' Then her eyes went dull. The death rattle followed all too soon.

'I didn't do it,' repeated Richenda.

Von Nacht looked past me. 'Take her away, Willoughby, and secure her. Stay by the room.'

Giles, our butler, came running down the corridor, a blanket in his arms. Von Nacht rose and took it from him. He cast it over Esmeralda.

'We shall need some men to take the body to a safe place.' Giles looked down at me. 'If you agree, ma'am?'

'Of course. One of the cellars should be cold enough in this weather. Please also light some candles beside the body and find someone who is happy to sit with her.'

'Of course,' said Giles and von Nacht together.

'Come away now, Euphemia,' said von Nacht. 'You must wash and change. I will meet you in the library and we can discuss what must be done.'

'Shall I telephone the police, ma'am?' said Giles.

I caught von Nacht's eye. 'I shall deal with that myself, Giles. You will have more than enough to occupy you. If any of the staff feel faint give them sweet tea. There will be extra compensation for those who are involved in dealing with poor Esmeralda.'

'No one would expect . . .' began Giles. Then he seemed to finally take in the great amount of blood that was spread about. 'Yes, madam,' he said.

Von Nacht took me by the arm and helped me to my feet. I was annoyed to find I was shaking. 'I should have sent for Griffin at once,' I said. 'He might have been able to save her.'

'Only a miracle could have done that,' he said. 'She had lost far too much blood. Bertram, will you help your wife?'

I turned to see Bertram, facing a crowd of curious guests. As ever, he had been holding the fort. I almost fell into his arms. Then I realised how bloody I was. 'She's dead,' I said to him. 'The poor woman is dead.'

Half an hour later, washed, changed, brushed and full of tea laced with whisky, procured by my loving husband, I entered the library. In the distance I heard the other guests quietly murmuring in the breakfast room. My stomach turned over at the thought of food.

I found von Nacht, not a hair out of place, waiting for me. He was alone. 'Where is Fitzroy?' I asked.

'That's a damn good question. I have no idea.'

I rang the bell. Willoughby responded. 'I thought it might be better if I oversaw any directions,' he said.

I nodded. 'Willoughby is here to help us,' I said to von Nacht.

He frowned. 'One of your footmen?'

'He works with Fitzroy and me,' I said. 'He was also at the front.'

Von Nacht shook his hand. 'This is a nasty business. I think we have no choice but to call in the authorities. As I have understood it from Fitzroy there might be a base here of some kind, but the majority of people present are usually civilians?'

'Yes, too many for us to simply give Esmeralda a quiet funeral in the local church. But I am also loath to call in the regular police, considering our guests,' I said.

'Can you call your office and make an arrangement?' said von Nacht.

'Ah,' said Willoughby and I as one.

'Please do not tell me he was acting unsanctioned?'

'Isn't that exactly what you are doing?' I said.

'Unofficially I have the Emperor's blessing. Does not Fitzroy have the same?'

'I fear not,' I said. 'But then I was not involved in the arrangements for this event.'

'What?' Von Nacht's polished veneer cracked as his voice rose. 'I assumed . . .' He smacked his hand against his forehead and turned to pace the width of the room. 'Fitzroy. Bloody Fitzroy. More slippery than an eel in butter.'

'Am I to understand that you believed this meeting to be at least unofficially sanctioned by SIS?'

'If not the King himself,' said von Nacht, pausing in his pacing, his forehead wrinkled with lines.

'Are you saying your Emperor believed this too?'

'I certainly led him to believe it.' Von Nacht slammed his hand, palm flat against a side table. It wobbled, but did not, as I expected, split in two. He opened his mouth to speak, but before he could there was a knock at the library door.

Willoughby opened the door, screening the rest of the room with his body. 'Might I speak to them?' said Griffin.

'Let him in,' I said.

'Please excuse this interruption,' said Fitzroy's major-domo. 'I thought Mrs Stapleford might like to know that there is nothing anyone could have done to prevent the death of the unfortunate young lady. The damage done by the knife was severe, but when the blade was removed it gave the blood free rein to flow. There is a slim chance she might have survived if she had had the weapon removed by a doctor, but it would have been touch and go.'

'Do you mean Richenda took the knife out?' I asked.

'I fear so,' said Griffin. 'I understand she was standing over the lady with it in her hand. It is, unfortunately, a most natural reaction to remove a knife from a living person. Generally, civilians believe it will ease the suffering.'

'Whereas it is the quickest way of killing someone,' said von Nacht. 'Any of the spies would know this.'

'Do you think it was some kind of accident?' I said, thinking aloud. 'She had a disagreement with someone, was injured, but before the assailant could fetch help, Richenda came upon the scene and withdrew the knife?'

'The simplest suggestion, I'm afraid,' said Willoughby, 'is not only that Lady Richenda withdrew the knife, but that she put it in in the first place.'

'She isn't a lady,' I said automatically. 'She is Mrs Muller.'

'A wronged wife married to an Anglo-German,' said von Nacht. 'I do not see how this can be kept under control without the help of your department.'

'Neither do I,' I said with regret. 'Please tell Fitzroy we need him at once, Griffin.'

'I fear I cannot, Euphemia,' said Griffin. 'I haven't the faintest idea where he is.'

Chapter Eighteen

Fitzroy's Inner Sanctum

Giles arrived at this moment to find us all standing around in shock. He took one look at us as he set the tea tray down, and murmured, 'Oh dear, I'd better fetch some shortbread.'

As the door closed behind him, I turned on Griffin. 'What? You mean he isn't in the house?'

'I don't know,' said Griffin, looking rather unhappy. 'I have a room near the servants' hall, so I do not know his comings and goings. He has not wanted me in his suite.'

'He has a suite?' asked von Nacht.

'He is here often,' I said. 'Because of the intelligence base – which you should not know about! He has his own suite he can lock to keep things secure.'

'But you have another key? A master key?' He looked from me to Griffin.

Griffin shook his head.

'I have a master key,' I said. 'I will go and check.'

'I will come with you,' said von Nacht.

'No,' I said, 'Griffin and Griffin only will accompany me. In the meantime, you and Willoughby can discuss what must be done, and contain the servants as necessary. How is the weather?'

'The snow ceased falling last night,' said Willoughby. 'A number of the locals have been out clearing the roads and pathways. We are no longer inaccessible, but we remain not that easy to reach.'

'They will have obliterated any footprints,' said von Nacht, looking grim.

I did not fully catch his meaning. My heart was quivering in my chest like a bird trapped in a cage. What if something had happened to Fitzroy? What if I never had the chance to tell him how sorry I was about our quarrel? I told myself he was most likely sleeping in after drinking too much, but the disturbance in the house would have reached him, wouldn't it?

I hurried to the stairs to his suite. Griffin took my arm firmly to prevent me from running. 'Things are bad enough without making them look worse, Euphemia. We must seem to be in control of the situation. Your guests are too dangerous.'

'Do you think he is unwell?' I said quietly.

'I have no idea,' said Griffin.

I unlocked the door to the staircase. He might have changed the locks, but I knew a good locksmith who copied keys for me discreetly. Griffin took pains to lock the door behind us. The short flight was carpeted with a deep blue material, quite unlike anything in the rest of the house, and the walls were painted a shimmering cream. 'He redecorated?' I said to Griffin.

'More than that, Euphemia,' he said, pulling a key from his pocket. 'He changed the locks on the inner doors too.'

'He did what? In my own home?'

'If it is of any comfort, I have never been in his suite. The key I have here was for dire emergency only.'

'So you think he may be inside, wounded?'

'I hope not,' said Griffin, slipping the key into the lock. 'But before I joined you I did a round of the house and nearby gardens. I could not find him anywhere.'

'Hurry up,' I said.

Griffin struggled slightly with the lock, but eventually it gave and the door swung open. He caught me by the arm as I moved forward. 'Be careful, I would not be surprised if he has not set traps.'

I looked down and indeed saw a fine line threaded from side to side of the doorway. 'Good God,' I said, crouching down. We both examined it, and came to the conclusion that the thread was too fine to pull something such as a pin from an explosive.

'This may just be to indicate if anyone has been inside,' said Griffin.

'Yes,' I said, but stepped over the thing all the same. Griffin did likewise.

We stood in a small entranceway with three doors leading off. One led to his bedroom, another to a private bathroom and the last to his study. I had expected it to be dusty, as Griffin had said he was not allowed here, but the space was spotlessly clean. On a small table stood an empty jade vase I had never seen before, and one of Fitzroy's many pens. There was also one of his chequered outdoor hats. I picked it up. The wool was rough, but dry. I lifted it to my face and smelt his familiar cologne, a mixture of cedar, amber and sharp pine. Griffin raised an eyebrow at me.

'You check the bedroom. I'll check the study,' I said. I had to tell him which was which.

I opened the door to the study and flicked on the electric light. I rather dislike its harshness, but it showed me in an instant that I was alone in the room. I had not been in this room since I handed it over to him. He had used his own people to move in the furniture. Being Fitzroy's, it was a lavishly decorated room. There was a large red Turkish rug on the floor, a small, elegant table on which stood a collection of decanters and glasses, a dark-brown writing desk with brass fittings and a lamp such as they have in banks, and a single wingbacked chair set by the fire. Logs were piled beside the hearth, which still held the embers of the last fire. These were stone-cold. I went over to the desk, and every single drawer was locked. The writing plane was completely empty. A few pens were lodged in the ridge along the top. There was nothing personal here, and yet the whole room was redolent of the spymaster. I thought I even smelled his cologne in the air.

I came out of the room to find Griffin in the hall. 'His bed has not been slept in,' he said. 'I checked the wardrobe. It's full of clothes.'

'Anything else?'

'A few books from your library. I should check the bathroom now. You should wait here.'

'I strongly doubt he has drowned in his own bath,' I said.

'Perhaps not,' said Griffin, 'but I would prefer it if you waited here.'

He opened the door, closing it behind him. I had barely taken a breath before he came out, opening the door wide behind him. I saw a scrupulously clean bathroom with a distinct absence of Fitzroy.

'He's not here,' said Griffin, stating the obvious.

'Then where the devil is he?' I snapped.

Griffin looked helplessly at me.

'At least tell me you have Jack in your room?'

'I'm sorry, Euphemia.'

Chapter Nineteen

Looking for Jack

'Well, that settles one thing. Wherever he is he'll have his dog with him. If we can't track the master let's see if we can track the dog.'

However, with all of the house opened up for the party, it proved quite the task to search for one small canine. Griffin disliked Jack almost as much as the dog disliked him. Even on their best days, Jack could conceive of Griffin being no more than a chew toy. However, Jack and I have always been on the best of terms. When I call, Jack normally comes running. Especially as all too often I have bits of sausage in my pockets for him. (It can make my clothing smell funny, but I think it is a small price to receive the dog's affections. Bertram is dead set against housing an animal of any kind except his horses. I believe Mrs Warburton still hides the kitchen cat when he is near.)

After a great deal of walking and calling, we finally heard a faint whiffle. Jack was happily ensconced in the kitchen, under the table, with a dish of leftovers. He lifted his head from his meal and gave me a happy grin in the way only English bulldogs can. The kitchen was all abustle for the meals that were to be served later today. I gave Jack a quick rub of the ears, and retreated with Griffin to the housekeeper's office, asking for Mrs Warburton to join us when she had a minute.

'He'd never have left that wretched beast behind,' said Griffin, sounding relieved. 'Perhaps he is involved in a . . . er . . . private situation.'

'And missed all the commotion? If nothing else he has a nose for intrigue.'

'Erm, yes,' said Griffin, reddeningly slightly.

'Besides, I counted heads when we looked for Jack at the breakfast table. Both Ruby and Lucy were there.'

Griffin's face grew a darker crimson.

'I know what he is,' I said, 'better than most.'

Griffin gave me a compassionate look. 'I'm sorry. It must be hard for you.'

I frowned. 'I don't follow.'

'Being a vicar's daughter.'

'Oh yes, but to be honest, it's harder to cope with the killing of adversaries.'

Fitzroy's major-domo started with alarm. 'You don't think—'

At this moment Mrs Warburton entered. 'Anything I can do for you, madam? Is it a change of menu?' She was wiping her hands on a clean cloth, and I could see they were rough and red with work.

'Oh goodness, no. I'd never do that to you at this late stage,' I said.

The cook smiled. 'Oh no, madam, I know you wouldn't do such a thing, but I thought one of those foreigners might be being difficult. What with one of them killing another.'

I goggled a bit at this. 'I'm sorry, the body must be putting you out of one of your cold rooms.'

'We'll manage, madam. We're all only glad it wasn't one of the family.'

'Thank you. I need to ask how Jack came to be under your table.' I raised my hand before she spoke. 'I know you can trust him to behave himself.'

'As long as he has his snacks, madam. I don't where such a little dog puts it all. But we all love him down here, and we know Mr Bertram isn't quite so keen, so I thought . . .'

'Very kind of you. But can you tell me how he came to you? Did Fitzroy bring him in?'

'Oh yes, early in the morning. He came through the kitchen so as not to disturb the house. He took the little fellow out to do his business. Then he came back in, looking for all the world like the abominable snowman. He said he fancied a bit of fresh air, but it was too cold for Jack, so could we keep him until he came back?' She paused. 'That would be some hours ago. We were baking the rolls for breakfast. Is he not returned yet? We thought he must have used the front door.' She looked worried.

'He's probably made his way to the Garden Hen for a pint,' I said, 'and got talking to the locals. He must be waiting for the snow to let up again.' I peered out of the small window at the encroaching blizzard. 'I take it it was milder this morning?'

'Clear as a bell,' said the cook. 'But you could smell the snow in the air. You'd think Mr Fitzroy would have been here enough that he'd got to understand the local weather.'

'Indeed,' I said, and steered Griffin out of the room.

'No footprints,' said Griffin.

'No.'

'I'll check outside for his car, and see you back in the library,' said Griffin.

'We'd have heard it,' I said, but I didn't stop him going.

We gathered back in the library. Willoughby and von Nacht had taken a head count of the guests and servants, and other than Fitzroy all were accounted for.

'Where's Bertram?' I asked.

'I believe he is attempting to get some sense out of your sister-in-law,' said von Nacht. 'I hope you will forgive us, but we have also confined Hans Muller to his room because of his known association with the deceased.'

It always shocks me how people lose their identity in death. One minute they are among us and the next we speak of them as 'the deceased', 'the body', 'the remains', or whatever else we need to use to disassociate ourselves from the spectre of death.

'We must discuss next steps,' I said. The faces gathered round the library table looked hopefully to me.

'As I understand it,' said von Nacht, 'is not Richenda Muller guilty of the murder? It was the act of withdrawing the knife that killed the woman.' He caught my furious look before I could respond. 'I mean no disrespect. I believe under your laws this would not be murder, as no harm was intended. Can we not put this down to death by misadventure and bury the poor lady?'

'We'd need a doctor's death certificate,' said Willoughby.

'I could,' I said, thinking hard, 'persuade our local doctor to sign a death certificate. He is under an obligation to me.'

'It would have to be a major obligation,' said Griffin disapprovingly.

'It is,' I said shortly, thinking how he had ruined Merry's life.

'What about the people in the house?' said von Nacht.

'I don't think they are particularly interested,' said Willoughby. 'Death is more a natural fact of their lives than ours. If you see what I mean.'

'We are overlooking the fact that there is a killer in the house,' I said.

'I would imagine,' said Griffin, his voice dripping in sarcasm, 'that the majority of the guests are already killers. Hence their nonchalant view of today's happenings.' Von Nacht raised an eyebrow. 'I have already seen more food being delivered to the breakfast room, and overheard more than one guest enquiring about luncheon,' continued Griffin. 'I do not think anyone is over-concerned.'

'There is the question of Fitzroy,' I said. 'We do not know where he is nor if he is safe.'

'Fitzroy is a big boy,' said von Nacht. 'He can take care of himself.'

'I am uneasy that there might be something else happening. Something we cannot see.'

'Possibly,' said von Nacht, shrugging. 'But is it not easier if we deal with this quietly between ourselves? I'm sure you have a local bobby who can also send in a report of death by misadventure.'

'We don't even know who Esmeralda is,' I protested.

'Hans Muller may have more information, but if not, we are all adept at creating legends, are we not?' said von Nacht. He rose. 'We have our answer. I trust your husband, Mrs Stapleford, can deal with the members of his family and the staff?'

'It's Lady Stapleford,' said Bertram, entering the library. 'What is this little cabal of spies concocting?'

I told him in bald language that could not be misinterpreted.

'No,' said Bertram.

'No?' said von Nacht, sinking back into his seat. 'What do you mean, no?'

'I mean,' said Bertram, 'that this is my home and it is run according to the wishes of myself and my wife. Unless you can say you want the matter of this woman's death swept under the carpet, Euphemia, I contend this death must be properly investigated for justice to be done.'

'Good God, man! We are in a time of war! The death of one insignificant woman—' said von Nacht.

Bertram cut him off. 'If we dispense with justice as and when it pleases us, all is chaos and the order of rule is lost.'

'Hear! Hear!' said Griffin.

'He does rather have a point,' said Willoughby.

Von Nacht turned in despair to me.

'I fear I agree with them,' I said. 'Not least because I feel we only have parts of the puzzle.'

'And if your Fitzroy killed her in a fit of passion?' snapped von Nacht. 'I imagine then you would overlook anything.'

Bertram flicked me a pained look. It was gone almost as soon as it appeared. 'He is not *my* Fitzroy. He is my partner in espionage, and he is as accountable as anyone else,' I said, lying through my teeth. There was no need for me to confirm to Bertram that I would kill, lie, steal and, in short, commit any crime to protect Fitzroy, and had already done most of these. Still, one must uphold one's principles in front of one who is not British.

'But who can we get to investigate?' asked Willoughby. 'It's true the local bobby would not suit.'

'Sadly,' said Griffin, 'I think I know the answer to that particular question.'

Chapter Twenty

Chief Inspector McLeod

I greeted Rory McLeod in the drawing room the next morning. Rory and I had a history. We have been servants together, and we had once been engaged, but I had jilted him. We had crossed paths during the war and had come to an uneasy truce. After being discharged from the army, he had entered the police and had more than once worked for Special Branch. He might still be doing so, because he had answered our appeal for help.

I came forward to shake his hand. 'Thank you for coming. Should I call you Rory or Inspector?'

His green eyes still had the inner glow that had first attracted me. His blond hair was as thick as ever. He was the only man I knew who made Hans Muller look plain. He was the most good-looking man I had ever met, and I hoped this earned me some forgiveness in falling for his charms.

'Rory between us,' he said, 'but Chief Inspector during the investigation.'

'Oh, a promotion,' I said. 'Congratulations.'

'There is more. I have also brought my wife with me. We are newly married and it is shortly before Christmas.'

'Oh,' I said again. 'Congratulations again. I look forward to meeting her.'

He smiled and nodded. 'Thank you. I shall keep her away from the investigation, but it would be a pleasure to introduce you afterwards.'

'She will not be disturbed being among a group of foreign spies?'

'I have no intention of telling her,' said Rory. 'And I would ask you to do the same.'

'As you wish,' I said.

'Now tell me everything and leave out no detail.'

We sat together in front of the fire and I told him the whole story with all its twists and turns.

'Hmm, and Fitzroy is still not returned?'

'No, now the snow has eased again I sent a man to the Garden Hen . . .'

'The public house?'

'Yes,' I said. 'They had not seen him.'

'Hmm,' said Rory, sitting back, his hands before him, fingertips touching. 'You realise there are a number of possibilities? Several of them unsavoury and possibly dangerous to you and yours?'

'Neither Bertram nor I killed her. I can swear he was with me. He's never been any good at sneaking around. Besides, you know he's not a killer.'

'I wouldn't have thought so, but I know he is fond of Richenda,' said Rory calmly. 'I think most policemen would follow the line that this is liable to be about the extramarital affair and focus on Hans and Richenda – and even Bertram and you.'

'And me?'

'I know enough about your world to know things are rarely what they appear to be. I would dearly like to have Fitzroy under my thumb. I would have expected him to ferret out any sordid details surrounding the lady – especially while he ran his event. I assume whatever plans he had, he did not inform Morley?'

I looked away into the fire.

'Why on earth did you go along with this, Euphemia? You must have known it was madness. That only one, possibly two, of you is dead seems a mild consequence compared to what could have been.'

My stomach flipped at his words. 'I did not arrange this event with him. It was between him and Bertram in England and him and von Nacht abroad.'

Rory lifted an eyebrow in a disbelieving way. 'Do you still have the letter that was sent to Richenda?'

I passed it over. 'I assumed you would wish to see it.'

'And you don't recognise the writing?'

I shook my head.

'What a tangle,' said Rory, running his hand through his hair.

'Why did you agree to come?'

He looked directly at me, that jade-green gaze fixing mine. 'Because you asked, Euphemia. I knew you would only call on me if you—'

'Wanted justice?' I said.

Rory nodded. 'Whatever bonds there are between us they will not stop me doing my job.'

'I know.'

'Good. I expected nothing less of you. I will manage matters with my superiors and depending on where this investigation leads, I will inform Morley should it become necessary. All you must do is tell me the truth.'

Chapter Twenty-one

The Prime Suspect

We began with Hans Muller.

Rory set up an office-style arrangement for himself in the main library. He seconded me to take notes for him. Hans sat before us on a straight-backed chair across a large library table. Rory had placed a large banker's lamp on the table, for the light remained dim. He had drawn me up a wingbacked chair, so I was slightly in shadow, and put out a comfortable chair for himself. The curtains were half drawn to keep some warmth in the room. It was only a little after midday. Rory had brushed aside any offer to let him settle in. 'My wife will arrange all that,' he said, reminding me why I would have made him a poor wife.

Hans paled in comparison to Rory's golden glory. He looked drawn, and his hair more yellow than blond. I noticed his usually impeccably manicured nails were bitten to the quick. He was smartly dressed, but sat on the edge of his chair like a naughty schoolboy.

Rory sat back in his chair, and spent a minute or more looking Hans over. Then he said, 'What I most need to know is if you knew Esmeralda before you met her on the train going north with Euphemia and the dog?'

Hans sat forward on the edge of his chair. 'No, you can ask Euphemia. It was a complete coincidence. Then the dog took a dislike to her, and I went to reassure her.'

'Your idea or hers?'

'Oh, mine,' said Hans. 'I try to be a gentleman.'

'That remains to be seen,' said Rory coldly. 'At what point did she become your mistress?'

Hans started back in his seat so hard, the front legs rocked up and then banged down on to the floor. 'You can't ask me that in front of Euphemia!'

'I just did. Kindly answer the question.'

Hans looked down at his shoes. 'Here,' he said in a quiet voice.

'Presumably before your wife arrived,' said Rory.

'Yes.' This time his voice was even quieter.

'Was this an arrangement made ahead of her arrival? Did you pay her? Or was it a seduction? And if so, by whom?'

Hans's head shot up.

'None of those. I made mention before, when we were in Scotland, that I was to come to Euphemia at Christmas. When I suggested she join us, I expected it to be a family event, and I hoped that she might make friends here. She was penniless and all alone in the world – except for an aged aunt and a miserly brother. Or brother-in-law.'

'You were planning on introducing her to Richenda?'

'I thought among family and friends she would . . .'

'Not obviously be your intended mistress?'

Hans opened his mouth to protest.

'How did you keep in touch after Scotland?'

'She wrote to me.'

'At your flat in London?' I asked. 'Richenda never goes there,' I explained to Rory.

Rory looked at me. 'Did you approve this dalliance?'

'Of course not. I thought Hans was spinning a story while we were on the mission. He had given her a false name, and I thought it was an enticement to, well . . . become closely acquainted with him. I know how much he likes to flirt.'

'And you did nothing to protect this young woman?' Rory frowned heavily.

'I was busy with the mission,' I said. 'And besides, I was most wary of her. I thought her likely to be a foreign agent who was leading Hans around by the, er, nose. I subsequently discovered she is not known to my department. I do regret that I didn't reach out to help steer her away to a steadier course. But in all fairness, even after, er, "bagging" Hans, the woman was flirting outrageously with other men in the party.'

'Who?'

I instantly regretted opening my mouth. 'We can discuss this later. You are interviewing Hans, are you not?'

'Who?' repeated Rory.

I sighed. 'Fitzroy. But I am sure there were others.'

'The same Fitzroy whose whereabouts are currently unknown?'

'Indeed.'

'Two of 'em,' said Hans beneath his breath. 'What a horrible thought. Two Fitzroys.'

'Was it Fitzroy who encouraged Esmeralda to come here, or was it entirely your own idea?'

Hans hesitated. 'Fitzroy led me to believe he had Euphemia's agreement.'

'And Esmeralda thought . . .?'

'She was being invited to a pre-Christmas party,' said Hans.

'You said she had no money?' said Rory.

'I sent her the fare to come here, and a little before.'

'Was she threatening to tell your wife?' asked Rory.

'No, besides, there was nothing to tell at that stage.'

'I see,' said Rory. 'One final question for now. What was Esmeralda's second name?'

Hans hung his head in his hands. 'Smith.'

Rory snorted. 'I doubt that exceedingly.'

Chapter Twenty-two

In the Soup

'He's lying,' I said after Hans had left the room. I rang the bell and requested refreshments. Rory looked over my notes.

'Your handwriting is appalling.'

I came and sat down again, edging my chair a little closer to the fire. It was extremely cold. Too cold in fact to snow again, and short of bundling myself up in a cloak I doubted I could be warm without sitting on the edge of the hearth.

'The thing is,' I said, 'Hans has had mistresses before, so I am certain he has ways of acting discreetly. He is also, through his own efforts, a wealthy man. I don't think the loss of a few notes due to the itchy fingers of a postman or two would distress him. I think he would think it worth the loss to keep it untraceable.'

'Does Richenda mind?'

'They didn't marry for love. I think she did expect him to stray, but there is a difference between him straying on a visit to town and bringing his infidelity to a family gathering.'

'Is that why you think he is lying?' asked Rory, pausing over one of the pages.

'Fitzroy told me he did not sanction her presence.'

'And you believed him?'

'He never lies to me,' I said.

Rory gave me a patronising smile. 'Of course not.'

'No, you misunderstand. It was an agreement we made long ago. He never lies to me. He might omit telling me things, but he never lies to me.'

Rory didn't actually reach out and pat me on the head, but his look said everything.

'Why would he invite her here? I mean Fitzroy. We wanted to keep the guest list discreet.'

'Why did he invite Hans?'

'Hans is intelligent and cognisant of what events in the world could mean. I don't mean he has access to secret material, but he has a shrewd mind. We needed people to help talk to the guests — to open diplomatic exchanges.'

'Is that what Fitzroy told you? You had said quite clearly that you were not involved in the arrangements for this event, and did not approve.'

Giles appeared with two bowls of hot soup, fresh rolls and some coffee. 'Mrs Warburton thought you could do with something substantial to keep you going till luncheon.'

I opened my mouth to thank them both, but Rory interrupted me. 'Thank you. Please arrange for lunch to be brought on a tray to the library. We will dine alone.'

'Very good, sir,' said Giles, giving the very slightest bow. He exited, closing the door with careful softness.

'Am I being interviewed?' I asked. 'Am I under suspicion?'

'Everyone is,' said Rory. 'But with Fitzroy missing, I want to keep my eye on you.'

'We are missing the opportunity to see how people gathered around the table react.'

Rory flicked a napkin across his lap with a practised ease. 'Dinnertime will suffice. Besides, you will be of more use here.'

I picked up my spoon and began to eat. I found myself very hungry. Rory ate slowly, and I was finished long before him. I poured the coffee and wished Mrs Warburton had added a few biscuits to the tray. I was considering ringing for some, when Rory said, 'I see the situation has not affected your appetite.'

'I am trained to eat when I can.'

'You really are a full and acknowledged agent then?'

I took the small token out of my pocket and showed it to him.

'I don't often carry it at home, but this . . .' I gestured helplessly around me.

'Help me understand what all this is about?' said Rory.

I told him once more Fitzroy's and Bertram's idea to open up the possibilities of peace. I told him of Fitzroy's experiences at the front, but not in detail. I did tell him some of the things Fitzroy had told me on our walk together.

'This does not sound like the man I know,' said Rory.

'He's complicated,' I said.

'Are you lovers?'

'Good heavens, no. He has become a family friend.'

'Hmm, your butler has said he is here often.'

'You've spoken to Giles?'

'I needed to ascertain who was in the house, and who had been in and out of the doors. Who else would I ask? He mentioned that you and another party member spent a long time in the garden together last night.'

'As the purpose of the gathering was to talk to people, I don't see anything odd about that.'

'He was very disapproving,' said Rory.

'I highly doubt he said anything of the kind.'

'He didn't have to say anything. You must remember how well I can understand people. Did I not tell you when we first met that I could always tell when someone is lying?'

'Yes,' I said. 'And I dropped a tray of food at your feet.'

Rory waved the comment away. 'My training with the police force has built on my natural talents. I am considered one of the more perspicacious officers on the force.'

'Congratulations,' I said.

'So, I am aware that both you and Hans Muller are lying. I just have to find out about what.'

We finished our soup in silence. I was offended. Rory paid me no attention. I suspected he was still trying to get things straight in his mind. Giles appeared with an unnaturally precognitive precision. He placed a small plate of biscuits at my elbow and withdrew, taking the tray with him. I bit into a biscuit. 'Such an excellent butler,' I said.

'I was better,' said Rory without the smallest sign of self-consciousness.

'And modest too!'

'Ah, having a meeker partner who values one tends to build up one's self-esteem, does it not?'

I almost choked on the crumbs.

'Come, summon him back. We must arrange our next interviews.'

'Richenda?'

'I doubt there is anything of use she can tell us. You have the note she received. As for killing the victim, she has had plenty of opportunity to confess and she has not. I can't think of anything else to ask.'

'What about when she found the— Esmeralda? Who else was around?'

'Oh, I am going to ask all those questions, Euphemia, but of your staff. I have noted how efficient a household you appear to run. Your presence with me should make them answer truthfully.'

'I remember now,' I said. 'You always were a cad at heart.'

Chapter Twenty-three

McLeod Behaves like a Cad

We worked our way systematically through my servants. Together with them Rory drew a precise map of the house, and pinpointed the guests' location before and after the event from their description. As all of the guests were in bed at the time this was not difficult to do. But as I watched him make his marks on the plan, I realised he was also encoding where the servants had been, and what they had been doing.

Willoughby was to be our next interrogee. 'He's one of our people,' I told Rory. 'Fitzroy must have put him undercover to watch the guests' servants.'

'Then I won't bother talking to him,' said Rory. He turned Willoughby away as he came to the door.

'If you don't mind me saying so, you are taking the strangest approach,' I said.

'I am interviewing British nationals only,' said Rory. 'Even your guests' servants are beyond my reach.'

'But how will you . . .'

'Achieve a result when I am so hamstrung?' said Rory, pulling over a small stool to rest his feet on in front of the fire. 'I may not be able to reach one. The times are too delicate for me to risk offending a foreign nation. I assume you have no Germans here?'

I shook my head. 'I believe Fitzroy had hoped . . . but no.'

'As was to be expected,' said Rory in a manner I found most annoying. 'Richenda and Hans have no investment in telling me the truth. I would expect them both, if either is guilty, to attempt to muddy the waters further. Perhaps even to protect each other.' He stood up and walked over to the small library humidor. 'May I?'

It was an odd time of day for a cigar, but I nodded. 'I'm surprised Bertram allows people to smoke around his books.'

'He believes it protects them from mould and silverfish.'

'Yes, you have chosen a damp and bleak part of the country to live.'

By now I wanted to argue with him about anything, but I could not bring myself to defend the Fens, which I loathed, and Bertram loved.

'I see,' said Rory. 'That makes your desire for adventure even more understandable. It is a great shame that you did not settle down and have a family like a decent woman.'

I shot to my feet, and would have done my best to do him an injury if Bertram had not ambled into the room.

'How is it going?' he asked. Then he saw my heightened colour. 'Have you distressed my wife, McLeod? Bobby or not, I will deal with you harshly if you—'

'I am sure I annoy Euphemia almost as much as she annoys me. However, I cannot tell you why she is currently so angered. I believe she was about to enlighten me when you entered. Euphemia?'

'You have no right to comment on how I choose to live my life!' I tried to sound as angry as I have ever done. I was hampered in this by the tears I was holding back as once again my lost child rose in my thoughts. Would I ever be able to overcome these heart pains? 'Only Bertram has that right.'

Rory laughed aloud at that, alienating us both, and putting Bertram on the offensive.

'You have had her company long enough,' said Bertram. 'My wife comes with me. She needs a rest before dinner. This has been very difficult for us all.'

Rory pulled a fob watch from his pocket and sprang it open. There was a clock on the mantelpiece clearly within sight. He appeared to study the watch face. 'I suppose I could allow that now.

I shall need to speak to you both again. Give me the notebook, Euphemia.'

'Don't get above yourself, McLeod,' said my husband through clenched teeth.

'That's Chief Inspector McLeod,' said Rory.

I was deeply impressed that Bertram didn't punch him in the face but instead offered me his arm so we could make a dignified exit together.

When we reached the sanctuary of our bedroom, I lay down without further encouragement. I felt suddenly bone-weary. Bertram rang for some tea, and then took up a position next to my side of the bed in an old wicker chair that he loved despite its awful, dilapidated state.

'So has he got anywhere?'

'No. I'm not sure it was a good idea to invite him,' I said.

'He had someone come and take the body away, which pleased Mrs Warburton. It should be a load off your shoulders. Fitzroy might have tried to handle this all himself, but you had the sense to realise we needed some support – authoritative support. He might have been a butler once, but he reeks of being a policeman now. It has calmed the staff considerably.'

'Oh well, that's something,' I said.

'Seems to have become a bit of pill though,' said my husband thoughtfully. 'I would say he had communist leanings, or socialist at least, only I've just met his wife.'

'What's she like?'

'You'll see,' said Bertram maddeningly. 'But she's the daughter of a duke.'

I stood up and stretched. I went over and put my arms around my comfortable, reassuring husband. 'I don't think the man can decide if he hates the class system or if he wants to climb it.'

Bertram squeezed me hard around the waist. 'Silly old thing,' he said. 'But then I always knew he had no sense. He let you go.' He kissed me, and for a time everything else vanished. It was only the two of us and everything felt familiar and safe.

Chapter Twenty-four

Richenda

After Bertram had a small luncheon sent up on a tray for me, and while Rory was away putting together his timings and movements, and the general observations of my staff, I went to see Richenda. I had a horribly long list of things I needed to do, and people I needed to speak with, and I had to prioritise. Talking to Richenda before Rory decided to drag her off to prison was a high priority. I believed she would tell me the truth, and I needed to know if she had killed Esmeralda. I pondered the line between civilian crime, the actions of war and the actions I had committed for King and Country. Sometimes the lines we drew seemed so arbitrary, but killing for personal revenge could not be acceptable. Richenda was capable of such an act. The question was, if she told me she had done it, would I protect her or would I see her hang? The thought made me shiver.

I knocked on the turret bedroom door and was relieved to hear her call from within. I entered. Richenda had a small table between the window and the fire. On it was a large cake missing a significant section that was on the plate in front of her. She paused, her fork halfway to her mouth as I entered. I noticed she had been given my best Chinese-blue china that I saved for special occasions. Clearly my staff didn't believe she was guilty. I only hoped that Rory was convinced by them.

'Cake?' said Richenda, gesturing at it. She gave me a bashful grin. 'It seems in difficult times I fall back on bad habits.'

I smiled and took a slice. It looked like one of the cakes I had planned for afternoon tea today. I sat down in the other chair. The fire blazed. 'This is cosy,' I said. 'I half feared Rory might have moved you somewhere less salubrious. I didn't ask him as I didn't want to give him ideas.'

'Rory?'

'Oh, goodness, has no one said?' I explained and told her about the discussions so far.

Richenda carried on consuming the cake at an alarming rate. She cut herself a second slice before answering me. 'It's not a bad idea to try and use the servants to work it out. I mean, they would have been up hours before any of us and might well have seen something.' She swallowed a large forkful. 'Bertram's told me about the spies and stuff. Diplomatic immunity, isn't it?'

'Possibly,' I said. 'Certainly, His Majesty's Police Force would not want to alienate an ally or even a neutral country in a time of war.'

'Gosh, it would be so dratted convenient if it was me, wouldn't it? No wonder McLeod is gunning for me.'

'I don't think he is,' I said slowly. 'I find him extremely irritating, and he is not allowing me to help him in any real way, but I think he is trying to do his best to find out the truth.'

Richenda pulled a face. 'It's a pity we didn't pay him better when he was our butler.'

I shrugged. 'That was before the war began. A very different time and quite erased by – all our experiences since.' I took a deep breath. 'But more to the point, what do you intend to do?'

'Do you mean do I intend to flee? Could you and your shady connections get me out of the country?'

'If you were serious, yes, but it would be unfair on the children – whether you left them or took them. Besides, the only place I could think of to send you is the Americas, and the journey is dangerous. I would not advise it. I could hide you in England, but again I do not think it is a good course of action.'

Richenda put down her cake fork. 'Do you know, I really think you could. Are you what Bertram calls "a master of espionage"?'

'Does he? How nice.'

'You've changed a lot since you were a maid in our household.'

'I should jolly well hope so,' I said. 'Now answer me. What do you intend?'

'About Hans? I don't know. I always knew there must be others. There were signs. But I could ignore the problem as long as it was out of sight.'

I helped myself to another, thin, slice of cake, and rang for some tea. I feared this was going to be a long conversation.

Later, I returned to our bedroom to dress for dinner. I found Bertram there struggling with his bow tie. 'Bloody thing!' he cried. Then he saw my reflection in the mirror. 'Darling, lovely to see you.' He turned round to kiss me on the cheek. 'You're frowning horribly. Has that dratted man been causing you trouble? Say the word and, if he has, I will deal with him.'

It took me a moment to realise he meant Rory. Generally the epithet 'dratted' or 'damn man' was reserved for Fitzroy. 'No,' I said, returning his embrace, and taking his tie off him. I went behind him and began to tie it. I was not much good at the task, but at least I was better than he was. 'I have been to see your sister,' I said. 'She wants to make up with Hans after all this is dealt with.'

'Really?'

'Stay still or I'll never do this! We had a long conversation and the long and short of it is that she feels affection for him and wants to have him around for the children.'

'Well, I didn't think she'd divorce him,' said Bertram with a bark of laughter, 'but I did think it might be one home, separate lives. Not sure I'd have him back in the marital sense.'

'Actually, that was one of the things that most upset her. When she opened the door and saw him and Esmeralda engaged with each other, she realised he was doing something he had never done with her, and she thought she would rather like it!'

'Euphemia,' said my husband, stepping away with his newly tied bow tie. 'You shouldn't tell me things like that! About my own sister. What was he doing?'

I burst out laughing. 'No, I shall not tell you.'

'It's not something that I, er, we don't do – and that you want to do, is it?'

'No,' I said. 'Nothing like that. She also told me she thinks she did kill Esmeralda.'

Bertram's legs went from underneath him, and he sat down on the bed. 'No!'

'Oh, no, not like that,' I said. 'Can you help me unbutton the back of this? She didn't stab her – although she does say if she had had a knife to hand when she saw her with Hans – er . . .'

'Quite,' said Bertram. 'Passion of the moment.'

'Quite,' I said, wondering why this was so hard to discuss with him. 'But she didn't stab Esmeralda. She says she found her leaning against the wall, about to collapse. She helped her lie down, and then saw the dagger.'

'Whose dagger is it?' said Bertram.

'One of the ones from the collection in the library.'

'Damn, I thought I was on to something.'

'Sssh, Esmeralda begged her to remove the dagger, so she did. Of course, that made the bleeding far worse and then she died.'

'So, the initial wound wouldn't have killed her?'

'Griffin said there was a very small chance she might have survived if a doctor had reached her before the dagger was . . .' I let my voice trail off.

'So, in a way, she did kill her, but not deliberately. How does she stand with the law?'

'I don't know,' I said. 'What she didn't do is ask Esmeralda what happened. She says she was too shocked to think clearly.'

'Pity,' said Bertram. 'Would have made all our lives a lot easier.' He took a step back to look at me. 'You look splendid in that dress. Positively regal. It'll annoy the hell out of McLeod.' He gave me a boyish grin and offered me his arm.

Chapter Twenty-five

Dinner

This was to have been our last night dining together, but circumstances and the slow clearing of the roads had inspired me to inform Mrs Warburton to prepare for another whole day at least.

Despite this, the dining table looked magnificent. Mrs T had set it with full crystal and our best serving set. The silver epergne with its palm trees and lions had been brought out, hiding little serving bowls that would be filled with sweetmeats and petits fours at the end of the meal. It stood some eighteen inches high and spread across a good three feet in width. It meant that those opposite each other got the merest glimpse of each other's hair. But then one never talks across the table at a formal dinner if one has been brought up correctly. Mrs T had also eschewed the new electric light in favour of candles. Their soft mellow light fell in golden pools across the table, except where it encountered silver or the diamonds on the guests, when it morphed into a myriad of winking stars, moonlight-bright. I should have overseen the table myself, but I had been too busy, and besides, I could not have done a better job. Perhaps the napkins could have been a subtler shade, but really, none of the men would notice such a thing, and I didn't in the least care what the women thought.

Bertram handed me into my seat. I smiled at those I could see and took stock of our guests. The moment I laid eyes on von Nacht, I determined to speak to him later. The man had aged a year if not more on this day. His distress was evident not only in his face, but in the few stray hairs around it. Yesterday he would not have dreamed of appearing before us so dishevelled.

Of the others, none that I could see seemed much perturbed. Mrs Mansfield had her knitting bag beside her. Gertrude and Mimi were eagerly reading the menu for this evening, twittering over it like hungry grey fledglings. Charlie was saying something to Ruby that was making her both blush and laugh. The two British Army men, who I must also grill, were deep in their wine already. The Grubers and the Smiths seemed to have formed an alliance. Lucy was coolly studying the new woman opposite her. The rest of the table was shielded from me by the wretched silver trees.

I followed Lucy's gaze and saw a small, bird-framed young woman, whose blond hair was piled high on her head. In amongst the locks were pinned more than one jewel. In an understated way she was pretty. It was the kind of prettiness that grew on you. The longer you looked the more you realised that her fine features were perfectly aligned and her blue eyes endearingly large for her face. She wore a gorgeous gown of pale-blue and silver lace. She kept her chin up, and looked about her, but I could see she also pressed upon the arm of her husband, as if reassuring herself he was still there beside her. Rory, of course, looked dashingly handsome without a hair or a thread out of place. From time to time he glanced down at his wife, even helping her adjust her chair. The expression on his face was that of someone who had something delicate and terribly precious in his care. She, when she looked up into his face, was all adoration. It made me wonder if I would be able to stomach my pudding.

Bertram dug me in the ribs with his elbows. 'Stop staring at Lady Jane,' he said. Not for me the tender looks. I muttered an ouch, but set about talking to Charlie, who told me extraordinary things about the price of vegetables during a war. The overall atmosphere in the room was much easier than one might have imagined. But these were not ordinary guests. Very few of them would be unacquainted with death.

When I rose at the end of the meal to lead the ladies out, I realised that neither Hans nor Fitzroy were present. I gave an inward sigh. Hopefully, they would be in the process of smoothing things out. How, I had no real idea.

Tea and cakes with the ladies was confounded by Lucy enquiring as to which game we would be playing this evening. When the faces of the other guests all turned to me with hopeful expressions, I realised another game was indeed expected by all. It seemed to have occurred to no one that sending people off to play some games when there was a murderer among us might be a bad idea. Internally, I struggled with the thought that the spies among us might even find it fun.

'How delightful,' said Mrs McLeod. I had still to be properly introduced. 'We always had such fun playing games at my father's house. Why don't we start with the Minister's Cat while we wait for the gentlemen to join us?'

'What is this game?' asked Mimi.

'Oh, it's delightful,' said Rory's wife. 'I shall start us off. I say: "The Minister's Cat is an awkward cat..."'

'How can a cat be awkward?' complained Mimi. 'Cats are graceful and lithe. Silent stalkers of the night.'

'In the night,' corrected Gertrude.

I slipped, like a cat, out of the room. I knew I didn't have long before I would be missed. I headed down to the kitchen, ostensibly to praise Mrs Warburton, but really to see if Fitzroy had had the same idea of meeting me away from the others. But he was nowhere to be seen. Instead, I found Jack still under the kitchen table. He lifted up his head when he saw me and gave a long low howl. The bustle around us stopped for a moment. I felt the hairs on the back of my neck stand up.

Mrs Warburton bent down and gave him a bit of something. 'Poor little thing,' she said. 'He must be missing his master.'

'What?' I said, alarmed. 'Is Fitzroy still not back?'

Chapter Twenty-six

I am Goaded into Doing Something Foolish

I suppose my response should have been to find my husband, but I immediately thought of Rory. It didn't matter how intelligent or informed Bertram was, he had no authoritative power. Rory, I thought, could at least organise a rescue party with trained men, who were used to searching in such weather. He must surely have such contacts.

I hurried up to the drawing room to find a merry scene. Rory's wife was chanting, while all the others clapped in time. I came in to hear, 'Xenophobic, yellow-eared, zesty cat!' There was tremendous general applause, and Lady Jane stood up to take a bow. Her pretty face was a delicate pink and her eyes were alight with fun and the room's appreciation. She seemed genuinely delighted that the ladies had enjoyed her game. However, the joy faded from her face as she looked towards me. As I too was smiling and clapping, I turned to see if the cause was behind me, and there I saw the door had once again opened and the gentlemen were waiting to join us. Prominent amongst them was Rory, his handsome face marred by a deep scowl.

'Bravo!' called Mrs Mansfield. 'Excellent game! Good show!'

The men surged past me to greet their ladies. Rory knocked my shoulder as he hurried past. I rubbed it without thinking. 'Are you all right, Euphemia?' asked my husband, appearing by my side. 'Want me to give that graceless cur a piece of my mind?'

'I doubt he would understand it,' I said. Bertram laughed. I turned to him. 'Did you know Fitzroy is still missing?'

Bertram shrugged. 'Man is like a bad penny. He'll turn up soon enough.' He must have read the concern on my face. 'You've told me that you've been trained to survive in difficult climates. I assume he was the one who taught you.'

'I know, but I can't think what would be keeping him away.'

'He was always rather fond of Merry,' said Bertram carefully. 'Do you think he went to visit her?'

'And stayed to help her with her predicament?' I said. 'In other times, perhaps, but not now, under the current circumstances.'

Bertram muttered something under his breath that sounded a little like, 'Not exactly what . . .'

'I don't know what else we can do,' he said out loud. 'We could attempt to form a search party of servants and guests, but how many of them would you trust?'

'Not to harm him?' I said, alarmed. 'You mean if he was already injured or hurt in some way? They are allies – at least I think most of them are.'

'You were right. It's a bloody stupid masquerade. Someone's already stabbed one of the blighters, and we still don't know who. Have you realised we might have some undercover Germans in the house?'

If Bertram hadn't figured out this was a key part of the whole secret identity plan, I did not feel like enlightening him now. 'I thought perhaps Rory might be able to organise some of his men.'

'Looks like he's in the middle of a matrimonial row,' said Bertram, nodding his head in the direction of a corner. 'Feel rather sorry for the pretty little thing.'

I looked across and saw that Rory was indeed standing over his wife. I couldn't hear what he was saying, but her head was lowered, and she had dejection written on every line of her form. 'He really is a pip, isn't he?' I said, and walked quickly over.

'Chief Inspector, Mrs McLeod, I hope you have been enjoying your evening.'

'It's the Honourable Mrs McLeod,' snapped Rory.

'Oh Rory, don't make a fuss,' said his wife softly. 'She's a baroness.'

'Are you?' said Rory in a surprised tone.

I nodded. 'Bertram doesn't like to use his title, so I generally don't either – and, before you ask, the idiotic will of the late Baron Stapleford was finally undone.'

'I see,' said Rory. 'If you might excuse us, I need to talk to my wife.'

'Did you know that Fitzroy is still missing?' I said, ignoring his dismissal of me.

'Is he? I'm sure he'll turn up somewhere, sometime.' He turned his back to me.

'I presume you have discounted him as the killer then?' I said.

He swung round at this. 'Are you seriously suggesting that Fitzroy murdered the victim and fled? Or are you trying to get me to arrange a search party for him? Because I won't do it.'

Mrs McLeod looked up in surprise at her husband. 'You mean a man is lost in this weather and no one has done anything to help him?'

'Don't interfere, Jane,' said Rory. 'These matters don't concern you. You've already drawn too much attention to yourself, when I expressly told you that you could only accompany me if you kept a low profile.'

'I think the ladies rather enjoyed your wife's game,' I said.

Rory gave me a furious look. 'Don't, Euphemia. Don't presume on our long friendship.'

Jane gave a little half-sob and ran out of the room, her hand to her mouth.

'Dammit,' said Rory, watching her go.

'She must really love you to be so upset by your disapproval,' I said thoughtfully.

Rory sighed. 'Whereas you have never been troubled by my disapproval or that of any other. I pity your husband.'

'Fine,' I said. 'We pity each other's spouses. Now what are we going to do? However much you personally dislike Fitzroy, you must admit his disappearance may not be a coincidence. For all we know, he went after the killer.'

'And is locked somewhere in mortal combat until we come to his rescue?'

He read the expression on my face. 'I need to talk to you anyway. Come back to the library. Bertram can organise this difficult house—whatever it is.'

I followed him, thinking at least there was whisky there. I reached for the decanter as soon as we entered. Fortunately, the staff had kept the fire burning and the room remained warm.

'You're turning into the spit of him,' said Rory as I poured my drink. I poured a second and passed it to him. He stopped complaining. I deliberately chose to sit by the fire before he could set us up at the table. Police, in my experience, value the expanse of a table in front of them. It makes them feel their authority. A fireside chat is quite a different thing. Rory moved towards the table, but seeing I had no intention of moving, he came, albeit grumbling, to sit by the fire.

'You don't know who did it, do you?' I said.

'I have found your staff to be honest – or they appear to be so, and with their detailed testimony of the whereabouts and habits of your guests, I am able to exclude some, but far from all.'

'All won't be much use,' I said.

Rory's voice became positively growly. 'You know what I mean.'

I set my glass down and turned to fully face him. 'Let us get something clear, Rory McLeod, your blustering and anger will not put fear into me. I am a very different person from when you first knew me.'

'I am aware—'

I put up my hand. 'You will not intimidate me as you clearly do your poor wife. I have killed men stronger and more skilled than you – in the service of my country, of course. Do not try me.'

'Threatening a policeman is—'

'What are you going to do?'

'About Fitzroy, nothing. About the murder, I must move on to your guests. I had hoped to avoid this, but I find myself with no choice. I can rule some of them out, but not all. I will need you to give your best indication of whom they may serve.'

'I will consider it,' I said.

'This is not a negotiation,' said Rory. 'There are two choices. Either Esmeralda was killed by Richenda or Hans due to the romantic triangle that had formed, or she was killed by one of your spies.'

'Why? Why would they kill her?'

'The only reason I can think of is that she too was a spy.'

'Nonsense,' I said. 'I checked up on her.'

'And you cannot be wrong?'

'Spies are dangerous,' I said. Rory sneered. 'I suppose she might have done or said something that . . .'

'Activated them?' said Rory. 'I doubt it. According to you they all knew the importance of this meeting. So, either one of your relatives is a killer or you're not as good at your job as you think you are.'

I swallowed the last of my whisky. 'It would have been a waste to throw that over you,' I said, and walked out with as much dignity as I could muster. Once in the hallway I again heard the echo of a howl from Jack. It was not as loud as before but filled with even more despair. I stalked back to the drawing room, not looking to see if Rory followed me or not. I dramatically threw open both double doors, startling the party into momentary silence.

'Gentlemen, one of our number remains missing. I suggest now that the snow has eased we form a search party. The moon is full and bright, and who knows if tomorrow will bring more snow? Who is with me?'

Chapter Twenty-seven

The Search

'You do know that most of them are half-cut, don't you, Euphemia?' said my husband. He was bundled up in a tweed cape, brogues, stout walking boots and wearing a deerstalker on his head with the flaps down.

I, too, had opted to wear a cape to conceal what most would consider shocking attire underneath. I needed the free movement. 'The cold will sober them up,' I said.

Bertram gave me a quizzical look. 'I can hardly stop them now.'

We stood in the corner of the main hall. Around us, men in cloaks and greatcoats struggled into hefty boots while our staff bustled around handing out packages of sandwiches and flasks of hot soup. Some of the ladies stood with their husbands twittering mildly and fussing over scarves. I was the only woman joining the party.

'What did Rory say that set you off?' enquired Bertram, selecting a sturdy walking stick. I made an exasperated noise. 'Being his normal self then,' said my husband with a chuckle. 'We'll have to work in a grid pattern. None of these chaps know the land. I've told the servants not to join in. Can't leave the house unsupervised.'

I nodded. 'I understand. Griffin is coming in case he is injured. Hans can't be allowed to come in case he absconds. I suspect Rory won't show.' I sighed. 'You're right, of course, he wound me up. But, on the whole, I don't think it was a terrible idea. Their genial mood as much as anything made them agree to come. Besides, if one of them has a bone to pick with Fitzroy and finds him injured, at least their intoxication will give him an advantage.'

'Has he such an issue with anyone here?'

'I have no idea,' I said. 'I don't know any of them.'

'Yes,' said Bertram thoughtfully, 'when you get into one of your pets you do tend to upturn others' plans.' Without another word he walked off to the front door. 'Gentlemen,' he said, 'let me explain how this will work . . .'

I reeled internally. Was any of this mess my fault? Bertram and I had made up – but I had only been at odds with him because of Fitzroy's cunning way of involving Bertram in his schemes. Really, I had had my husband's best interests at heart. My husband who at this moment was most effectively organising a group of drunken foreign spies into a search party.

I felt something wet on my hand. Griffin had come up beside me. He had Jack on a lead. 'You wouldn't like to take the White Demon, would you? He's already tried to bite me twice. He might be of use in the search.'

I bent down and rubbed Jack's ears. He snuggled at my hands. 'Of course,' I said.

'I wouldn't normally bother with a lead, but I was afraid he might fall into a snowdrift – and then you would feel obliged to pull him out,' said Griffin. I thought I heard a faint regret in his voice.

We set out around ten o'clock at night. The moon was bright and full enough I felt no need for a lantern. Not so the rest of the group. Almost at once we were turning back for lanterns and hastily made torches. I did not take one, and moved to the side of Bertram's formation so they would not blind me. As I watched Charlie Bingham gaily trip down the steps, I realised that he was one of the ones who had indulged at the decanters. I took an even further stance away from the group. Whisky and fire was a bad combination. I began to regret my idea.

The bitterly cold air sobered our group. The cheery chat that had filled the hallway dwindled to no more than people confirming their position; a regular call-in, so we knew no one had stumbled into a ditch. The wind nipped at noses, reddening them, and chafed with needle-like cold at any exposed skin. One of the Smiths' sons, who had retired behind a wall to deal with a call of nature, arrived back shocked and pale. I assumed he had run into a sheep.

Our country is flat. There are no hidden summits. We have curated the local forests, building them up, as Bertram believes the roots hold the land together against the water. He has caused many small walls and dykes to be built, so the estate is a mixture of deep woods and banded fields. Next to the house itself is a huddled group of buildings: the old mill, the church, the doctor's cottage and several smaller dwellings. A little further on are our stables. The local public house stands between the farmworkers' cottages. There is a maze of pathways, worn by feet, and only one proper road out leading to the wider world. In the snow it looked picturesque, but it is a confusing landscape that easily turns one around. And there are the marshes – everywhere and where you least expect them – they are deadly.

At one point, as we came across the summer field, Mr Gruber, round as a ripe beetroot, staggered on the stile and only the quick reflexes of Mr Smith saved him from ending up in a ditch. Bertram, who had witnessed this, said in a low voice, 'Serves him right. Man has most of my best port in him. Utter sponge.'

It quickly became clear that, despite Bertram's clear instructions, the group had already begun to fall apart before we had walked a mile. The cold might have awakened them, but it also confused them. Some of them had put on greatcoats but had not changed from their evening dress beneath. Others found themselves slipping and sliding over the frozen surface of the snow. They had expected the powdery snow one finds when skiing and not the ice-hardened rink that confronted us. Willoughby made good progress with a kind of sliding gait. However, when the Colonel and his Lieutenant tried to follow suit they quickly ended up on their backs. There was a small tussle with what seemed like far too many arms and legs as the Smith sons tried to make themselves useful in righting the men, only to fall themselves. I watched mesmerised for a few moments. No sooner was one up than another was down. Then I realised how cold I was and carried on.

Von Nacht drew up beside me. 'I think you should bind that dog's paws,' he said. 'He is already limping.' He offered me a handkerchief. 'The best I can do,' he added.

We told Bertram, and fell back to a wall that gave some shelter from the wind, to bandage Jack's paws against the cold. I felt dreadful.

'I think we should turn back,' said von Nacht. 'I want to find Fitzroy as much as anyone, but we may have accomplished all we can tonight.'

'We have gone no more than a few miles.'

'Which is a lot further than I expected. It is a testament to your husband's organisational ability. I have studied the others as much as I can when they are so bewrapped, and I have seen no sign that anyone is reacting – I mean, knows which way to go or why this might be pointless. I assume that was part of your reason for this?'

'One thought,' I said. 'We will also have time to observe them when we return.'

Von Nacht nodded. 'We are also making enough noise that if he were out here, he would respond and we would hear. There is not much more to be done, unless you wish to lose one of these fools to either exposure or the marshes. If so, let me know who, and I can hurry them along. Like Jack, my extremities grow cold.'

'If you hold on to Jack, I will find my husband,' I said.

I found Bertram quickly. He was rushing back to me. Red-faced and panting, he gasped, 'I've found Jenny!'

Chapter Twenty-eight

A Kingdom for a Horse

'Who the devil is Jenny?' I asked. 'And what is she doing out here.'

'She's a horse,' said Bertram, still puffing from having made his way quickly to us. 'I had no idea she was missing from our stables.'

'Really, Bertram—' I began.

Von Nacht cut me off. 'Is she the kind of mare one would take hacking in the country?'

Bertram nodded. 'She's in the Harpers' field. For all we know, old Fitzroy is tucked up in there with a broken leg.'

'But why would they not have got a message to us?' I asked.

'Old couple,' said Bertram. 'Two of their sons are away at the war. Only a young girl left. Probably waiting for the weather to improve.' He gave a sigh of relief. 'You and I should go up and have a chat,' said Bertram. 'Griffin and von Nacht can show the others the way back.'

'There are footprints,' said von Nacht, disparagingly.

'They are drunk,' said Bertram. 'Hot toddies all round when we get back.' He clapped his hands together happily.

'We can't turn up on these poor people's doorstep in the middle of the night,' I said.

'I should imagine with all the noise we have made they are already awake. Besides, there are some stubborn characters here, and they will not turn back until there is some sign of success,' said von Nacht.

'Won't leave the mission, what?' said Bertram jokingly.

'Exactly,' said von Nacht. 'I will spread the word around that you are engaging with a possible target and see if I can ship them back with Griffin's help.'

'Shouldn't I go with you; in case he's injured?' said Griffin.

'Oh, very well,' said Bertram. 'I'll go home and supervise the blankets and whatnot.' He did not look too disappointed about this.

Griffin and I picked our way across the muddy track to the little farmhouse. I could feel my heart beating faster in my chest. We had no need to knock on the door, which swung open at our approach. I had been heading towards the kitchen door, and had to reorient slightly, catching my foot in a frozen rut. I would have fallen if Griffin had not caught me. I could feel my ankle beginning to throb with pain, but I smiled and hurried forward. To be welcomed at the front door was to be an honoured guest. It was also the middle of the night, and we had obviously been making enough noise to make it clear we were from the big house.

Mrs Harper, with her long grey hair neatly pinned up and wearing one of her best blue dresses, welcomed us. She spoke with a strong local dialect, but both Griffin and myself had become accustomed to this and hardly heard it now. 'Welcome to our house, ma'am, sir,' she said. 'My husband has a little stiffness getting out of bed and begs you will excuse him coming down a bit tardy.'

'There really is no need for him to come down,' I said.

Mrs Harper closed the door behind us and led us through to a tiny perfect parlour. It was spotless. The fire was newly lit and still weak but coming in from outside it was very welcome.

'Please sit. I will fetch a pot of tea and some bread and butter.'

'There's no need,' I began, but Griffin elbowed me hard in the side. 'Tea would be lovely,' I said. 'But please do not feed us. I know how hard things are.'

'Bless you, my lady,' said Mrs Harper. 'We might be short of jam and sugar, but we always have the best butter and bread. We farmers share among ourselves, as well as with the big house.'

'Now, wife, mind your tongue,' said an elderly man, hobbling into the room, leaning heavily on a stick. 'We've got enough explaining to do as it is.'

I stood up to greet him. He waved me back down. 'No need to stand, your ladyship. Especially not after what we've done.'

I must have looked mystified. 'An explanation is the better for a pot of tea,' he said. 'You must be Mr Griffin. I heard how you helped the Simpsons out with their sow.'

Griffin blushed slightly. 'Oddly, the body of a pig and of a human are not that dissimilar. I was happy to help.'

'I'm sure the good Lord knew what he was doing when he made the pig. I'm not so sure about when he made man.' He looked thoughtfully into the fire. I ran my gaze quickly along the mantelpiece to check for black-lined telegrams.

'Have you heard from either of your sons?' I asked.

The old man nodded. 'Billy got sliced up by shrapnel. They must have some damn fine doctors over there. They got the worst out just behind the lines. He's been shipped back to one of the ports. He couldn't tell me where. Just said he had a Blighty one and was coming home. I think one of his legs is damaged, but he's still got both. Thank the Lord. Not sure how he'll be able to work on the farm. But we'll see. Rather have him back broken than not at all.'

Mrs Harper came back in carrying a tray. 'Our younger son, David, has had a battlefield promotion. He's a sergeant now.' She looked very proud. Griffin jumped up to help her with the tray. Then came the pouring of tea and passing round of sliced bread with thick creamy butter. Having been trained by my mother to handle the trials and tribulations of high teas at noble houses, I could more than cope. Griffin, however, had more difficulty. Mrs Harper took pity on him and brought through a rough stool from the kitchen to use as a little table. 'Be a shame if he ruined the rug,' said Mr Harper. 'Paid a pretty penny for it.'

The firelight and one smoky lamp revealed a little of a floor covering that seemed to have every colour of the rainbow worked into it. I remarked on its loveliness, and both the Harpers relaxed a little back into their chairs. I could hear no other sound. I knew they had a young daughter, but only serious illness would have prevented Fitzroy from joining us. I began to fantasise – the worst two possibilities were that he was dead in their barn, or he had run off with the daughter.

'About the horse,' said Mr Harper after we all had a second cup of tea poured. 'We were always going to return it.'

'I don't doubt it,' I said.

'Oh, thank the Lord! When we heard you all shouting outside, we thought we'd got it wrong, and it was some kind of fancy racehorse.'

I blinked. 'No, it's a nice mare for riding. She's not strong enough to do fieldwork. And she's certainly not of racing stock—'

Griffin interrupted. 'We were looking for the rider,' he said.

The Harpers looked at each other. 'She weren't saddled when we found her,' said Mr Harper. 'We thought she had escaped from the stable. Spooked maybe. Neither the wife nor I ride anymore, so we were going to get Mary to bring her back once the weather cleared a bit. She's not that confident on the horse.'

'Of course,' I said. 'That makes perfect sense. But there was no sign of anyone having been nearby?'

'Horse had strained its fetlock a bit. I put a poultice on. I reckoned she come a cropper trying to jump over a wall.'

'But there was a rider?' said Mrs Harper.

'I'm afraid so,' I said. 'He has been missing two – three days now.'

'Riding bareback,' said Mr Harper. 'It weren't Mr Fitzroy, were it?'

'Yes,' said Griffin eagerly. I reeled from the knowledge that Fitzroy knew my tenants better than myself.

'Oh dear, I hope he hasn't come to any harm,' said Mrs Harper. 'Such a nice gentleman.'

'And you're only looking for him now?' said Mr Harper.

'We thought perhaps he had business elsewhere,' said Griffin.

'Business 'e could reach on a horse in this weather?'

I stood up. My heart had returned to its normal speed and made its way down to my boots. 'We are most sorry for disturbing you,'

I said. 'I will send someone to collect the horse and reimburse you for the feed.'

'No, no, I don't be wanting any of your money,' said Mr Harper. 'Only doing what any neighbour would do.' The unspoken criticism hung in the air that he should have started searching for Mr Fitzroy some time ago.

'Oh no,' I said. 'I was thinking we could replace the hay and the ingredients of the poultice. We certainly owe you that. This is turning out to be a most harsh winter.'

Mr Harper's frown faded slightly, and he nodded. Mrs Harper rose to see us out, but only after we had politely and repeatedly refused more offers of tea, or even a spot of breakfast. Apparently, Tam Wills had brought over a bit of the pig he'd just slaughtered for them. I pretended not to hear this as Mr Harper threw dagger looks at his wife. I let Bertram run the farms, and what was our due in various divisions was quite beyond me. Seeing how simply and how proudly these people lived made me inclined to not take a penny from them, ever. But then the whole estate did have to run.

I was musing on this as we walked down the path to the fields.

'You're limping,' said Griffin.

'Turned my ankle,' I said.

'Do you want to lean on me? I'll look at it when we get back.'

Thinking that had Fitzroy been around, Griffin would not have dared be so friendly with me, I put my arm around his neck and let him take some of my weight. It helped a lot.

'He wasn't there,' I said.

'No,' said Griffin. 'Tomorrow in daylight I'll get someone to go back and look at where they found the horse.'

'Good idea,' I said, and burst into tears.

Chapter Twenty-nine

Facing the Most Unpleasant Facts

The next morning I rose late. Bertram went down to host breakfast and I stayed in bed resting my ankle and getting my emotions under control. I lay in bed with my leg raised and tried to think of where Fitzroy might be. There had been an occasion once when he and I had been caught out in the freezing cold in a car that had stopped working. He had been badly injured and he tried to prepare me for the inevitability that I would have to go on alone and leave him behind – in the knowledge that he might die. I had refused to do so, and against the odds help had come. I feared that this time no help had come for Fitzroy and that he had died injured in the snow. If only he had taken Jack with him. I was sure the little dog would have fought to get help for his master. How could he leave me in this position? There was so much happening and he was gone. I felt tears trickle down my cheeks, and turned my head into the pillow so no one would hear me sob.

I came down mid-morning using an improvised stick. I went to the library. Rory was there, as I expected, poring over some papers. He stood up when he saw me and pulled out a chair. I took this to mean I was no longer a suspect.

'I am yet to interview anyone this morning,' he said. 'I thought I would wait for you. It's all rather delicate. I now also have to consider if the absence of Fitzroy is an intentional act.'

'If he'd meant to kill Esmeralda she would have died at once.'

Rory winced. 'I meant could it be that someone deliberately

brought him to harm? His absence lends credence to the possibility that this is somehow – espionage-related.'

He said 'espionage' as if the word was a wasp in his mouth.

I nodded. 'So how do we proceed?'

He frowned and peered at my face. 'Have you been crying? I wasn't aware that you could cry.'

I gave him a half-smile. 'My ankle is very sore.'

'Rubbish, you'd take a bullet and not complain. Why are you so upset over Fitzroy?'

'He's my partner. We've saved each other's lives a score of times. You become close.'

Rory nodded. 'I might not have understood that before I went to war, but I do see it now. I will, however, always think that such a partnership should not be between the sexes. It is all too easy for such relationships to become entangled.'

'Really, this is not the time or place to criticise me. I am emotionally distraught enough to bounce that paperweight off you.'

'That would be a serious crime,' said Rory firmly and without humour. 'Attacking an officer of the law.'

'Don't worry. I would aim for your head where there would be least damage to be done.'

I waited to see his reaction. There was a pause, and then gradually, as if he could no more hold it back than hold back an incoming tide, a small smile appeared on his face. The difference when Rory smiles is like night and day. His whole countenance and bearing changes. The stiff formality vanishes. His green eyes seem to glow, and he becomes a person who emanates a trustworthiness and an openness that is rare.

'You should smile more,' I said. 'People would respond to you more positively.'

'Hmmf,' said Rory. 'In this job I am not in the business of making friends.'

'Are we friends?'

The smile diminished slightly. 'We may become good acquaintances. Married men do not have female friends.'

I nodded, not wanting to open up that debate again. 'I should get to know your wife.'

'That would be suitable,' said Rory. 'But before you distract me further, let me explain who I have managed to rule out of harming Esmeralda from your servants' testimonies.'

'Did you hear about last night's events?'

Rory sighed. 'Tell me.'

I summarised the situation precisely.

'Why was the missing horse not noticed?'

'Bertram is checking with the stables this morning.'

Rory shuffled the papers in front of him. 'So, your servants report that the two army officers stay up late smoking and generally keep themselves to themselves. They are often late for breakfast and always in each other's company.'

'It would be easy enough to establish a routine so that when one secretly breaks it . . .'

'It leaves one out of suspicion. I had worked out that much,' said Rory. 'But the fact they are always together makes it less likely they are involved. We're looking for a single killer. Are they British Army?'

'I don't know. Before you ask, I don't know who Charlie Bingham is either. I'm quite mystified by all of them.'

'Would von Nacht know?'

'Possibly,' I said. 'We should get him in and ask him. I see no reason why he would not comply with the request.'

I rang the bell and asked the maid who answered to ask Baron von Nacht to join us. She immediately ducked her head as she giggled and blushed. I frowned and she hurried out.

'You had no need to describe him,' observed Rory.

'She has clearly noticed him,' I said, privately thinking it was likely to be the other way round. The maid was a pretty little thing, not quite nineteen years old. Her large blue eyes and her surprisingly curvaceous figure must have drawn von Nacht's attention. I recalled at that moment that although Fitzroy would give female staff compliments, he distributed them equally among the women, regardless of age. I had never seen or heard of him trifling with a servant's affection. Von Nacht was like a darker version of my partner, and I needed to remember that. On the surface they might resemble one another but, for all his more handsome features, von Nacht was the lesser man. It was, I reflected, looking into the fire, rather a disappointment. He had smelled extremely pleasant.

'Thoughts?' said Rory, dragging me back to the present.

'Don't trust von Nacht. He is loyal to the Austro-Hungarian throne. Charles the First, the new emperor, wants to help bring about peace. Not least because he is afraid his own empire is on the verge of collapse.'

'Is it?'

I shrugged. 'Possibly. But the Ottoman Empire is liable to go first,' I said in a knowledgeable way. Although I had no real idea. Thus are such rumours made that bring about the fall of kings.

Von Nacht arrived promptly, dressed in a dark day suit without a hair out of place, and his shoes as shiny as a mirror. His cologne entered the room before him. 'How can I be of assistance?' he asked, clicking his heels together and bowing slightly.

Rory indicated that he should pull up a chair. 'I understand you were one of the masterminds behind this event?'

Von Nacht nodded and helped himself unasked to the whisky even though luncheon was yet to be served.

'It may be,' said Rory carefully, 'that the murder of Esmeralda Smith – does anyone know her real second name, by the way? No one I have asked has been able to provide it – anyway, that the murder is not the result of a matrimonial dispute, but rather something that stems more from your world of espionage.'

'Because Fitzroy is missing?' said von Nacht, at once grasping the point. 'If he had wanted the girl dead—'

'I know,' said Rory, interrupting him. 'But what if someone has brought him deliberately to harm?'

Von Nacht paused. 'Of course, one has considered that, but I have not been able to establish any facts that might lend credence to that solution.'

'Your English really is very good,' I said, impressed despite myself.

'English nanny,' said von Nacht. 'I am unsure what else to tell you.'

'I have begun to rule out people,' said Rory. 'The servants report that the Smiths never go anywhere without their three sons.'

'Yes,' said von Nacht, taking a sip of whisky. 'I do not believe them to be offspring, but rather a personal guard. You have seen the way they move, Euphemia? Do you not agree they are fighters?'

'I suppose one could train one's sons to fight,' I said. 'But the fact they always stay together, I assume for fear of assassination, means they are unlikely to have hurt Esmeralda. As for Fitzroy, I don't know.'

'Ottoman Empire,' said von Nacht. 'I don't think Fitzroy had any particular, what do you say, "beef" with them.'

'The Grubers,' said Rory.

'French. Fitzroy might have paid the pretty little wife too much attention. He likes blond women.'

Rory adopted a fierce frown, doubtless thinking of his own petite fair-haired wife. We continued on through the guests until we had a list. It looked like this.

- *The Smith party (Bulgarian, confirmed by von Nacht), always all together. Unlikely to have killed Esmeralda. And no reason to think they were related. No known argument with Fitzroy.*
- *The Grubers (French). Thought by servants to be abed when Esmeralda murdered. Had asked for milky coffee in bed. Mr Gruber annoyed with Fitzroy for flirting with his wife.*
- *Lucinda Scarlatti (Italian). Suspected to be with Fitzroy during murder (von Nacht). Feels scorned by Fitzroy?*
- *Winifred Mansfield, partner to von Nacht, vouched for.*
- *Col. Long, Lt Wools. Unknown in all respects.*

- *Charlie Bingham (another branch of British Intelligence?).*
- *Ruby Milton (Ottoman Empire spokesperson?). Jealous of Lucy? Also flirted with Fitzroy.*
- *John Groats (American). Brash man, not making any friends. Assumed observer only.*
- *Mimi and Gertrude (Russian – which side? White or Bolshevik?). Very frail. Unlikely either would have the strength to kill a healthy young woman. Even when working together.*
- *Willoughby (ours). Soldier turned spy with bad shell shock. Protégé of Fitzroy. Disagreement.*
- *Von Nacht (co-organiser of event). No known motive to harm either.*

'Thank you,' said Alex.

'Unless, of course, you felt Esmeralda was endangering this event?' said Rory.

'Same goes for him as Fitzroy,' I said. 'He is an effective assassin when needs be.'

Alex von Nacht bowed his head in my direction. 'Thank you.'

Rory considered us both, the expression on his face torn between amusement and disapproval. He leaned back in his chair, his eyes on our list. 'What about the rest of the house party?'

I jotted down some notes.

- *Fitzroy. Not known for killing women, effective assassin. Missing.*
- *Bertram (ex-SIS). Incapable of killing. Dislikes Fitzroy but has recently begun to get on better with him.*
- *Alice (SIS). Experienced assassin. Partner to Fitzroy.*
- *Hans. Not a natural killer, overwrought at being caught out. Might have blamed Fitzroy.*

'Now there is an idea I had not thought of,' said Alex.

- *Richenda. Stayed at the scene. Heat-of-the-moment temper, but more likely to blame Hans than Fitzroy.*
- *Giles (butler). Old before his time, very traditional, would never have left a mess. Dislikes Fitzroy.*
- *Mrs T (housekeeper). Horrified at Esmeralda's presence, murder would be an even worse social faux pas. Very fond of Fitzroy.*
- *Mrs Warburton. Rarely leaves realm, no knowledge of Esmeralda other than as an extra guest to be fed. Almost as fond of Fitzroy as she is of Jack.*

'I feel this is getting a little whimsical,' said Alex politely. I took my gaze from the paper, and saw Rory's expression. 'I was trying to add in some colour,' I said. 'No one is ever black or white.'

'A lot of this is opinion,' said Rory. 'Like your claim your husband couldn't kill anyone. Not even in defence of his sister's honour?'

I shook my head. 'Wouldn't that mean Hans? I can see him punching Hans, but I believe they've been talking, and Bertram is being a go-between for him and Richenda. You have to understand,' I said to Rory. 'It was a marriage of convenience for both of them. Hans might have tried to conceal his affairs from Richenda in the past, but he never concealed his nature from her.'

Rory gave a little shudder. 'Next you will be telling me this is all normal for your class.'

Alex gave a small shrug. 'Maybe not normal, but not infrequent. Traditionally marriage is about alliance rather than love. Once the first two heirs are born, it is not unusual for the spouses to seek companionship elsewhere. Does Hans have an heir?'

I nodded. 'One son, and two daughters. He has told me he wishes them to inherit equally.'

'So, something of a maverick?' said Alex.

Rory pushed himself away from the table. 'It must be almost luncheon. I need to think about what we have here. We also need to ask people again if Esmeralda told any of them who she was.

Or, in fact, gather anything she told people. We don't even have a second name for her. I will see Hans again, alone. Someone must know more about her than they are saying.'

'All she said to me when she was dying was, "It was a good game."'

'She'd lost a lot of blood,' said Rory. 'I doubt she knew what she was saying.'

'Do you consider Fitzroy's disappearance and Esmeralda's murder to be separate crimes?' asked Alex.

'Normally, I'd say the likelihood of two murders occurring in the same party is remote. However, this is not a normal group of people. I don't intend following up on Fitzroy's absence any further. Euphemia is more than capable of organising searches, and until she turns up a body, I am unwilling to call in resources to help us.'

'A body,' I said, starting. 'You mean you think he is dead.'

'Euphemia, if I may,' said von Nacht. 'Fitzroy would not willingly absent himself from this event. It is possible he is held captive, I suppose, but he is a resourceful operator. Every day he is missing makes it more likely he is dead. You will need to face this.'

I felt lightheaded and dizzy. They had to be wrong, but before I could open my mouth to speak, the luncheon gong sounded.

Alex offered me his arm. 'Allow me to take you into luncheon. I will find a quiet place for you to sit and think.'

Chapter Thirty

What About the Germans?

'Doesn't someone have to represent the Germans?' I asked Alex softly. We were sitting at a small table together. As before, the luncheon had been put out like a buffet. Alex had chosen a table in full sight of the others, but slightly further away from the main throng, where we were less likely to be overheard.

'We had hoped so, yes,' said Alex. 'Are you asking if a German spy might have harmed your partner?'

I nodded. 'They tortured him before. His hands.'

Alex lowered his head. 'Ah, yes, I remember. He was an Olympic-level shot, but no more. That was a great pity. You rescued him, did you not?'

'There were a few of us.'

'But you were the one who would not believe him dead? I hate to tell you this, but I do not believe any German spy or anyone here would hold him hostage. What would be the point? He might think himself so important, as you know,' he gave a small smile. 'But he is not worth the price of peace.'

'So, what do you think has happened to him?'

'I think he fell from his horse, injured himself and has not been found. It is not likely after such a time that he is still alive. His horse may have lost its footing in the snow, and he fell headfirst, and died at once. I think that would be best, don't you?'

I wanted to say I would know if he was dead. I wanted to say that our bond was too close for me not to know, but I feared sounding either like a hysterical female or his mistress, or both.

'What do you want to do about your plan?' I asked, trying to concentrate on what really mattered. My heart might be hurting so badly that I could only take small breaths lest it split asunder, but I knew so were those of the wives and mothers of the soldiers who were fighting and dying for what was becoming a war that was as horrendous as it was without end.

Alex patted my arm approvingly. 'You had it right, when you asked about the Germans. I told your Inspector Rory what I thought, but I still hope to be wrong.'

'You mean that the Germans are here? Fitzroy thought they might be the Colonel and Lieutenant?'

'It is not inconceivable,' admitted Alex. 'As for what I intend, I will carry on with the plan. Only now I must ask for your help. Fitzroy and I had divided up the parties between us. We intended to draw them aside and have intense conversations with them. Tonight, he was to have talked with Ruby and Charlie Bingham. Would you take this charge? I will be talking to the American and the Smiths. Winifred is talking again to Mimi and Gertrude, and she will also speak with Lucy. We can compare notes at the end of the evening, or in the morning. Whichever works best for us all.'

'What do I ask?'

'There is not enough time to brief you on everything that has gone before. This may be no bad thing. You come to the discussions afresh. You ask them their views on the war and how it could be ended.'

'That blatant?'

'Remember,' said Alex, pouring me another glass of wine, 'that they have not declared who they are speaking for. They stand as individuals giving their own opinions.'

'And Fitzroy?'

Alex gave a deep sigh. 'Order whatever searches you can with your own people. Listen to see if anyone mentions him, as I will too. That is all we can do.'

'And Esmeralda?'

'Is inconsequential to our mission. Let the inspector handle that.

And perhaps suggest he should do his own job instead of involving you. Your mission matters. It matters more than anything you have ever done and quite possibly more than anything you may ever do.'

I heard the noise of a chair scraping. Bertram was dragging one over to our table. In one hand he clutched a piled plate. He put it down awkwardly on the table, so some of his olives rolled on to the tablecloth.

'Dash it! Sorry, von Nacht, Euphemia. Didn't quite have enough hands.'

Alex dodged an olive that attempted to roll into his lap. 'I am only grateful you were not carrying a pudding with custard,' he said.

'Ah, yes, or hot soup! Ha! Ha! Quite see your point. Not really the thing for the hosts to sit together at this sort of thing, but I had to tell you what I discovered. It's the most dashed thing.'

'Oh,' said Alex, as he reached into his waistcoat pocket for his monocle. He screwed it into his eye socket. 'Now you see me at my most serious.'

Bertram gave him a look that said he wasn't sure if he was joking, but Alex kept a straight face. 'Turns out it was old Fitzroy who told the stableboy not to tell anyone he'd taken the horse. Tipped the lad a shilling too. He's been beside himself not knowing what to do.'

'It didn't occur to him that the rider might be hurt?' I asked.

Bertram shook his head. 'It's little Archie. The Patersons' boy. Hard worker but not very bright. They couldn't trust him alone on the farm, so I said we'd find something for him. Turns out he has rather a gift with horses.'

'Ah, a horse whisperer?' said Alex.

'Yes,' said Bertram, 'but not a terribly intelligent one. Got all mixed up about who he owed his duty to and all that. Picked up something was going on in the house and got it into his head that Fitzroy was a secret soldier going off to war.'

'Maybe less dim than you think,' said Alex. 'Could we talk to him about how Fitzroy was when he left?'

Bertram's food was piled wobblingly high on his fork. He stuck it quickly into his mouth and held up his fork to suggest we waited a minute. 'Thought of that. I was on the intimidating side. Though perhaps Euphemia could do it. Take Jack. He's all right around horses, isn't he?'

'Yes,' I said. 'You think Archie will be calmed by the sight of an animal?'

'Much more than a person. Loves his ma though. Respects her,' he said through another mouthful. 'Firm and kind, I'd play it, with Jack for extra reassurance. He'll be in for his piece and a cup of tea in about twenty minutes. He eats in the boot room. Finds the servants' hall too noisy.'

'Then if you will excuse me, gentlemen, I had better change into something more suitable for this meeting and find Jack.'

'You won't forget what I asked?' said Alex.

Bertram mumbled something through his food, which I imagined was an enquiry. I smiled brightly and swept out of the room.

Chapter Thirty-one

Archie the Informant

It is a wearisome necessity that one has to change several times a day when one has guests. Also I knew the boot room to be always somewhat dirty. No matter how many times the scullery maid swept it out, a moment later someone from delivery boy to stable-boy would tramp through, bringing half the countryside with them. Really, it was as if these delivery people took it as a mark of pride to make the place as muddy as they could. Or that is certainly what Mrs Warburton believed. I only registered that it was yet another of White Orchards' inconveniences that all those passing through the back door also passed through the boot room.

I chose one of my hardier dresses that could stand a stiff brushing-out of mud and dirt. I liked the colour, a deep indigo, but the fabric was thick enough to itch when one got warm. It would be no great loss to have it out of use for a few days.

I found Jack under the kitchen table being spoilt by Mrs Warburton.

'Can't bear to turn him out,' she said, feeding him one of Bertram's favourite pork-and-apple sausages. 'His eyes. So sad. It'd take a crueller soul than me to shoo him away.'

I bent down and petted Jack and fondled his ears. He gave a little shake of the head as if to say, Not now, I'm eating my sausage. 'But it's not ideal to have him in the kitchen,' I said. 'I think Mr Bertram would be rather upset if he knew.'

Mrs Warburton became crestfallen. 'I do know he is not keen on the animal.'

'Around food,' I said. 'Neither am I. He should not have been left with you. I have a little errand for him then I shall take him to Mr Griffin to care for him.'

'He says the dog bites him.'

'Well, if nothing else that will cheer the little beast up. Come on now, Jack. Time to come out from under the table.' I took a couple of raw sausages from the table. 'If you don't object, Mrs Warburton?'

Jack followed me, if not happily, then with his attention firmly fixed on the sausage links. The boot room was empty, so I settled Jack on the floor and found a perch to sit on. It was no more than a few minutes before a boy of thirteen or so entered. He had bright-red curls, freckled cheeks and an open and friendly demeanour.

'You must be Archie,' I said. 'Go and grab your food from Mrs Warburton and then I'll introduce you to Jack here. I've got some sausage you can feed him.' He looked at me with a glazed expression. 'It's all right,' I said. 'I'm Mrs Stapleford.'

Understanding dawned on his face. He gave his flat cap a little tug, pulled off his boots, and ran in stockinged feet into the kitchen. I noticed there were large holes in his socks. When he came back I patted a seat next to me. He had a hunk of bread and cheese on a tin plate and was grasping a mug of tea in the other. I helped him put the mug somewhere safe, thinking perhaps I should have had Mrs Warburton prepare the sausages for him and not have brought them for the dog.

As he ate, I said, 'This is Jack. He loves having his ears fondled like this. He loves sausages. Eats them raw!'

Archie swallowed. 'That's right. Some animals like to eat meat. It's good for them. Not horses though. Nor cows.'

I nodded. 'That's right. What about you, Archie? Do you like sausages?'

'No, ma'am. I won't eat another animal. Ma says it's OK to eat eggs as they're not yet anything, but I can't eat another living thing. It would choke me.'

Archie didn't strike me as unintelligent so much as different. 'Does Mrs Warburton understand?' I asked.

He grinned at me with a mouthful of cheese. 'Says it's more chops for everyone else.' He downed the rest of his tea. 'Can I pat the dog now, ma'am?'

'His name is Jack, and yes, you may. Here, feed him this.'

Whether it was the food or not, Jack and Archie took an instant liking to each other. In a few minutes the boy had Jack doing tricks – turning round and lying down in return for pieces of sausage.

'You certainly have a way with animals,' I said. 'You've cheered him up. This is Mr Fitzroy's animal. You remember him? He took a horse out riding.'

'I hope as I didn't do too wrong not saying,' said Archie, frowning heavily, and biting his lip to hold back tears. 'Only I gave my word.'

'You're not in trouble,' I said, thinking what would make sense to him. 'I think if there ever is another time someone asks you not to mention them going out riding and they don't return, you should tell us for the sake of the horse.'

Archie nodded seriously. 'I heard they found her, but she has a sore leg.'

'It'll mend,' I said. 'Could you please tell me exactly what Mr Fitzroy said? Only he is a friend of mine and I'm worried he might be hurt. Did he give any indication where he was intending to go?'

Archie scrunched up his face and spoke slowly. 'I came in and he was talking to the dog – Jack – saying how he couldn't go as it was too cold. He told the dog that he'd never felt so hurt by – Alice – and something about you couldn't trust anyone now. Then he must've heard me as he whipped round, and he looked right angry. Scary angry. But then he saw it was only me. Hello there, Archie, he said. Don't you mind me. I'm in a rotten mood. Can you be a grand lad and not tell anyone what you heard or saw? Then he gives me a shilling and asks me to make sure the dog didn't get out. Which I didn't need to do as he told it to stay, and it did.'

I swallowed hard. 'I see,' I said. 'Thank you for explaining it to me. Was that all he said?'

'He might have told Jack more before I came in, but only Jack knows and I don't speak dog anywhere near as well as I speak horse.' There was no trace of humour on his face when he said this, so I merely nodded.

'How would you feel about taking care of Jack for the rest of the day? You can take him to Mr Griffin when it's his bedtime.'

'When does he go to bed?'

'Same time as you,' I said, thinking quickly.

'I'd love to, ma'am. Can I show him the horses? Does he like 'em?'

'I believe he does, but be careful in case the horses don't like him.'

'Oh no, ma'am. My horses know to behave themselves around my friends.'

I left Jack with him, and heading back through the kitchen, asked Mrs Warburton to ensure that Archie got extra milk, cheese and eggs as he didn't eat meat. Then I hurried upstairs to change my dress. It wasn't especially dirty, but I needed time to control myself. Fitzroy had gone on that ill-destined ride because of me and my threat to telephone Morley. It was all my fault.

Chapter Thirty-two

And then there were Two

I don't remember how I got through the rest of that afternoon. I avoided Rory as I knew I would give him short shrift. Fortunately, he didn't call on my services. Neither did he start interviewing my guests. Giles, finding me in my own boudoir in the afternoon, told me that Inspector McLeod had asked for access to the telephone in private. I surmised he was enquiring of his superiors how much power he had in this situation. Diplomatic consequences and diplomatic immunity issues must have had him strongly conflicted. On the other hand, calling for further support from his superiors made it all the more likely that Morley might hear about this. It wouldn't happen automatically. One thing I had learned about departments like ours was that they tended to have as little to do with anyone else as possible. I thought of it as a sort of hubris-driven snobbishness. Only we knew what we were doing, and should we let anyone else know they would be likely to mess it up. Fitzroy, naturally, had taken this approach to extremes.

Fitzroy. I could not get the image of him lying somewhere in the snow, slowly dying, but watching the horizon for the sight of me coming to his rescue. I could order the servants to search again, and I would do so, I decided, in daylight tomorrow, but I was mortally afraid of what they would find. I suspected Alex was right, and the odds of him being alive were very slim, if they existed at all. But then Fitzroy had beaten worse odds before. All I could do for now was to do as Fitzroy had wanted and try to talk the others into launching a peace initiative.

At pre-dinner drinks I indicated to both Ruby and Charlie Bingham that I would like to chat to them afterwards. I suggested without quite saying that I wanted to discuss what Rory was doing, and how they felt about being lined up for interview. Both seemed intrigued by the individual invitations, and happy to meet.

We were embarking on the fish course, turbot somehow magically produced by Mrs Warburton, when all hell broke loose. I had been vaguely aware that someone had rung the front doorbell, but I hadn't given it too much thought. I was far too preoccupied watching the interactions at the table.

But then I heard loud voices in the hall. Whoever had come to the front door seemed to have gained access to the building. I had a horrible thought that Morley or some other official might be here in answer to Rory's call for assistance, and that they might be coming to close the event down or – worse – arrest us. Giles materialised by my side. 'Madam, you must come at once. The most extraordinary thing has happened.'

I rose at once. I noted that Giles seemed more surprised than worried and did not waste any time asking more questions. I nodded to Bertram, who frowned and nodded back. I hoped he realised I meant he need not follow, but short of shouting down the dining table there was little else I could do.

I hurried to the front hall, and there saw two well-dressed country gentlemen I did not know and – Fitzroy!

He appeared uninjured and was in the process of unwrapping himself from his outer garments, which were heavy with snow. 'You must take care to dry these properly,' I heard him say earnestly. 'My constitution is not strong and it will not do for me to put on a damp coat. Thank you, Ann.' Our little maid nodded and gave a small curtsey, as if this was the most normal thing in the world, although everyone in the house knew he had the constitution of an ox. Then he turned back to the other gentlemen, who were also divesting themselves of their coats and handing them to Mrs T. Both of them appeared hesitant in doing this and were looking around the hallway, a little alarmed. It is often only when guests enter White Orchards that they realise how large it is.

'Come, come, gentlemen,' said Fitzroy, gesturing at them to hurry. 'You are our most welcome guests. There is a large party at the house here, as I told you, but we will have our repast separately in the smaller dining room. Our cook is excellent, and you need warming after such a journey!'

I stood watching him as if I was somehow outside the scene – as if I was in a dream where I could observe but not act. I was torn between delight, I admit this, that he was alive, and fury that he could not have contacted me. More than that, he had arrived back with no warning and with extra guests when our house was at bursting point already!

Then he saw me. His face lit up as if he had turned into the sun. He strode towards me, and before I knew what he was about, swept me into his arms and kissed me heartily.

I didn't try to free myself immediately, which I had to explain to Bertram in detail, because at first I realised that this must be a dream. Also – and this I did not admit to my husband – he was a superb kisser, as I had always suspected. A gentleman cannot have such success with the ladies without having the necessary skills.

Behind me, I heard the angry cough of my husband. Fitzroy finished his embrace but held me close with his arm around my waist. I then saw, to my horror, that most of the dining room had followed Bertram into the hall.

'Hail and well met,' said Fitzroy. 'I apologise for giving you all such concern, but I am returned hale and hearty. I must also beg your allowance of my behaviour. It is too many days since I have seen my beautiful wife.' At this point, he hugged me closer and planted a kiss on my cheek. Bertram assumed an explosive expression. 'Sir,' he uttered, 'Will you be so—'

I finally managed to wake myself from my stupor. I gently extracted myself from his arm. 'I shall look after your guests, my dear, but will you be so kind as to allow Griffin to examine you? You must have had an accident.'

'Of course, my dear,' said Fitzroy, looking down at me with love in his eyes. 'I was going to suggest the same myself.' He was magnificently uncaring about his audience in a very Fitzroy-like manner, but I knew he was not himself.

Griffin, who had been lurking somewhere ineffectively, now came forward and took Fitzroy away. I asked Mrs T to take our guests to the small dining room and provide for them. Alex shuffled people back to the dining table, and I turned to face my husband.

His face was an alarming beetroot colour, and his fists were clenched at his side. He finally gave vent to his feelings. 'The man cannot be right in the head!'

'Indeed, that is exactly what I fear,' I said.

Chapter Thirty-three

The Imposter

The rest of dinner was a hurried affair with most of the guests declining dessert. When the ladies withdrew, I gave my apologies, and asked Jane to lead a new and interesting game for the tea-drinking. She smiled in delight. I hoped her husband would not blame her.

Bertram too abandoned the guests, leaving them under Alex's charge. Rory, unasked, also joined us. We found Griffin waiting for us in the library.

'What the devil is going on?' said Bertram as soon as he saw the hapless manservant.

'Perhaps you would like to be seated,' said Griffin in his best professional manner. He had, after all, once been a respected doctor. His demeanour was serious enough that we complied, although Bertram grabbed the decanter and a glass for him and me before sitting.

'As you have observed, Fitzroy is not himself,' he began.

'I should say so,' said Bertram. 'He kissed my wife in front of me. I should have his head.'

'Ah,' said Griffin, 'the problem with that is, he doesn't actually know he offered you insult.'

'What are you blabbing on about,' said my husband, who is usually unfailingly polite.

'I think I know,' I said. 'He has suffered a blow to the head, has he not?'

'Doesn't know what he is doing?' said Bertram. 'Bally convenient. Don't believe a word of it!'

Rory, I noticed, had a small superior smile on his face. Unfortunately, Bertram was between us or I would have kicked him hard on the shin.

'Mrs Stapleford has it correct,' said Griffin. 'He has not only suffered a blow to the head, but the force has rearranged his memory. He believes himself to be Bertram Stapleford.'

'What!' said my husband.

'Knowing him as I do, I conducted some exhaustive tests, and it is my professional opinion that he is under the delusion of believing himself to be you, Bertram.'

Rory gave a bark of laughter.

'Then we must disabuse him of this illusion at once,' cried Bertram.

'It is my hope the situation will naturally rectify itself over the next few days.'

Bertram swore and made it very clear he was not prepared for this to take days and was more than willing to go and explain the situation himself to Fitzroy right now. He threw in a few descriptors that I had previously heard from Fitzroy, but had had no idea my more nicely spoken husband knew.

'It would be very dangerous to do so,' said Griffin. 'I have noticed of late that Fitzroy has been in a very overwrought state. He is phenomenally intelligent. I have lost count of the languages he speaks fluently. I am far from aware of all his skills, but I know he is also a master codebreaker and strategist.'

'Jolly good,' said Bertram. 'Sounds as if he is smart enough to sort himself out without any help from us.' He got up. 'I'm off to see to our guests. Someone has to.'

'If you please, not so fast, Mr Stapleford. I am afraid that for the sake of Fitzroy's health I must beg a favour of you.'

A look of wariness and suspicion crossed my husband's face. He frowned and his lips twisted slightly. Anyone else might have thought he had indigestion, but I knew what this meant. 'I make no promises,' he said.

'If you would retake your seat I could further my explanation,' said Griffin.

'No,' said Bertram. 'Something tells me I would be better off facing this standing.'

Griffin took a deep breath. Rory, who hadn't said a word so far, or even taken a seat, propped himself up on the mantelpiece as if he was the master here, and looked down his nose at Griffin.

Griffin spoke to me directly. 'If Fitzroy sees the person he thinks he is, I believe his mind would be in danger of breaking. There will be a reason he has decided to be your husband . . .'

'Yes, and I know exactly what that reason is,' said Bertram.

'You know, Euphemia, how much he has been struggling since he last returned from the front. He is fragile.'

'This isn't your speciality, is it?' said Rory, speaking up for the first time.

'No, not exactly. I have been reading about the science of the mind, but it is very new.'

'So, you're not an expert,' said Bertram.

'No, but I have some training in this area, and as I said I have been reading—'

'Reading,' said Rory in a disdainful tone. 'When will Fitzroy be able to tell us what happened?'

'Possibly never,' said Griffin.

'You mean he is going to think he's me forever!' snapped Bertram. 'That is intolerable.'

'If he is to come to his senses I would expect it to take place naturally over the next couple of days.'

'If?' I asked.

'There is always the possibility that he has suffered too much – both in potential concussion and in psychic trauma.'

I felt fear run through me like quicksilver. 'But he knows too much,' I said. 'He could . . .'

'Never be allowed to go to an ordinary hospital,' said Griffin. 'He would have to be locked away in an institution.'

I saw Bertram's lips twitch, and I had to restrain myself from throwing a book at him. Then he gave a huge sigh. 'I suppose we can't have that happening to the old chap. But look, I'll stay out of his line of sight, but I'm not going to lock myself in a cupboard.' He tugged his moustache decidedly. 'And I am not, I repeat am not, going to change my sleeping arrangements. I don't care what you have to do to him – sedate him, knock him out, but there are ways in which he bloody well won't replace me!'

My cheeks grew hot and scarlet. Rory gave another bark of laughter. 'Very well,' said Griffin, 'we have a plan, such as it is. I will be on hand to supervise, and we will hope this situation falls out in good order.'

'Hmmpf,' said Bertram.

Chapter Thirty-four

Fitzroy Escapes

We decided we had no choice but to tell the others what had occurred. Their reactions ranged from indifference to annoyance, and in Alex's case deep concern. 'It's always the great minds that break. I don't think most people realise how intelligent he is.'

'It's his impetuousness,' I said sadly. 'He can go into a very orderly and mathematical mode, but most of the time he is doing things as he thinks of them.'

'You mean he never plans a mission?' asked Alex incredulously.

'Oh, of course. But no plan survives contact with the enemy, does it?'

'This one certainly didn't,' said Alex, scowling.

'So, you do think this is an action by an enemy state?' I said.

'If you mean the Germans,' said Alex, 'I have no idea. I have not definitely identified any German agents. Have you?' He included both Bertram and me in his glance and ignored Rory. Rory seemed to sense he was excess to requirements. He got up, saying with as much dignity as an ex-butler can manage, which is quite a lot, 'I shall start my supervision of the subject. You will need to make yourself scarce, Bertram.'

'What, you mean you are going to give him free rein of the house? We don't even do that for our chickens!'

'As I understood Griffin, he is to be allowed to act as he wishes.'

'Damn this,' said Bertram, standing. 'No, von Nacht, I've not confirmed anyone to be from Germany. We have suspects, but you and Euphemia can work that out for yourselves.' Bertram then exited the room before Rory, and with even greater dignity – which was on the verge of regal. Rory followed him out quickly.

'Looks like things are up to us,' said Alex.

'Grand,' I said, not meaning it in the slightest. 'So, I imagine you still want me to talk to—'

I didn't get to complete my sentence as Fitzroy burst into the room. 'Can you believe, Euphemia,' he cried. 'I've missed both ruddy dinners. I've sweet-talked Mrs Warburton into giving me something in the small morning room, of all places. Still, I suppose it will be morning soon. Come and keep me company and eat a roast potato or two.' He paused. 'At least I hope there will be roast potatoes. Do you think there will be?'

'Oh, there have to be,' I said, rising. Fitzroy nodded approvingly. I gave Alex a look that was meant to signal I was handing things over to him. Honestly, it was quite a relief as I had no idea how to take things further.

Fitzroy took me by the elbow and more or less pulled me out of the room. 'Come on, my love. I've got Griffin on my tail. I think there's something up with the poor chap. Probably wants to ask me a favour. Maybe he wants to get away from the bad man and come into service with us. Ha! That would be a laugh, wouldn't it?' His eyes sparkled as he said this, but his colour was high, and he was speaking far too quickly.

'Let's get you some food,' I said, starting to walk towards the room. Fitzroy, still attaching himself to me, followed.

'Absolute mess of a plan that man arranged. A dead body and parlour games! Is that what you would do normally when working for the Crown?'

'Not usually,' I said. There was a small table set for one in the morning room. Surrounding it were a host of lidded pots from which a number of enticing smells arose.

'This won't do!' said Fitzroy at once. He pulled the bell hard. Giles appeared in moments. 'Giles, old chap, can't leave the lady standing, can we? Set a place for my good lady, will you? And I hope there's roasties in one of them pots.'

'Of course, my lord.'

'Oh, come now, none of that,' said Fitzroy as Giles looked at him, stricken. 'I don't believe in all that nonsense. Sir is perfectly fine. It's more than time we started breaking down the class barriers. We're asking young and old to die alongside their so-called betters. We are all in it together. We need a much more equal system.'

Giles's jaw dropped, but he hurried off to fetch the extra cutlery. Fitzroy insisted I sat in his place and began to investigate the dishes. 'Looking good,' he said. 'Can I serve you something?'

'I have already eaten.'

'You're as pale as a goose, and thin as a broom. You need feeding.' He piled some potatoes and small Yorkshire puddings on my plate and splashed them all over with thick gravy. 'Unctuous stuff!' he said.

Giles returned quickly. He bent to whisper in my ear. 'I didn't realise he was so ill,' he said. 'Socialism! He may need to be confined.'

I smiled and waved him away.

Fitzroy attacked his food with great gusto. His fork only seemed to stop moving when he was gesturing to me to eat. 'Tell me everything that has happened while I was away. I hear there's been a death. It wasn't that man, was it?'

'No, and that's a dreadful thing to say.'

Fitzroy frowned. 'You're fond of him, aren't you?'

'Yes. We're partners. We've been through a lot together.'

'I'd be careful,' said Fitzroy. 'I'd trust you to the end of the earth and back, but that man's bad. He'll break your heart.'

'It's not like that,' I said.

'Rubbish! I see the way he looks at you. Man's in love with you.'

Considering who was speaking I was lost for words.

'Tell me everything,' he repeated, so I poured out the details of everything that had happened since he had been gone. 'You have been having fun, haven't you? What did you find in Esmeralda's room?'

'I don't know what Rory found.'

'Good gracious, Euphemia, you can't leave it to that half-trained plod! And as for that man, he'd probably go sniffing in her underthings drawer! We must make haste and go up!'

Chapter Thirty-five

The Room of the Dead

Someone had drawn the shades in Esmeralda's bedroom, I presumed out of respect. Fitzroy bounced in behind me, and turned on every light he could find. 'The thing is,' he said, wrenching out a bedside cabinet drawer so hard that it fell on the floor, 'that one must do these things methodically.' He looked down at the drawer. 'Goodness, Euphemia, I think we need to look at upgrading some of the furniture. This stuff is not fit for purpose.'

'Perhaps you could be a little gentler?'

'Nonsense. I am only using reasonable force.' He left the drawer on the ground and went on to open the wardrobe and pull out all the drawers in the tallboy. This time, at least nothing came away in his hand or fell to the floor.

'A brief glance tells us nothing unusual here,' he said, eyeing the mess. 'Help me lift the mattress, and then we can have a go at the trunk at the end of her bed. Interesting it wasn't taken away like the other guests' luggage.'

I struggled to lift my side of what proved to be a well-stuffed mattress. 'She wasn't expected,' I said between puffing and panting. 'And we hoped she would go at any time.'

'Yes. Yes. Quite,' said Fitzroy, dropping his end of the mattress. 'Nothing there. Maybe I should use my penknife on the thing. It was damned heavy.'

'Only if you can spot where she might have sewn it over,' I said quickly. He already had his instrument out of his pocket.

'Very well. I appreciate you don't want to damage the furnishings, but we may have to. Let's have a go at that trunk. Ring the bell and get Giles to bring up a crowbar.' His eyes lit up at the thought of the destruction he was about to inflict.

I went over to the trunk. I tried the lid, and it lifted easily. 'Good spot!' he said to me with a smile, but I could see the disappointment in his eyes.

I knelt down beside the trunk and began to sift through it. It seemed that Esmeralda had either been unsure if she was going to stay or else had been too hesitant to ask one of the maids to unpack.

'It's all as one might expect,' I said. 'Oh, wait a minute. She has some thick socks. Odd, for a woman.' I unrolled the pair. 'No, nothing inside. I suppose they could be worn under a long dress if one had particularly cold ankles.'

'And hot thighs,' said Fitzroy with a crack of laughter.

'I suppose they might have been a present for Hans. They feel a bit odd.'

Fitzroy froze, rather dramatically, beside me. 'Hand me a sock,' he said with the seriousness of a surgeon asking for a scalpel. 'And ring for a pail of water at once.'

I stood up. 'Do you want to shave?'

'Just do it, woman. Have it brought here.'

One of the maids brought a pail in short order. 'Thank you. Thank you. You may go,' said Fitzroy, taking the bucket and shutting the door behind her. 'I wonder if we will be able to see it,' he muttered.

'There's enough light to land an aeroplane,' I said.

Fitzroy dropped a sock into the water and stared at it.

'What do you expect to happen?' I asked.

'Ssh,' he said. 'We may need a stick.'

'It is an attack sock?' I asked, wondering if he was losing his mind.

'Don't talk nonsense, Euphemia. Hang on!' He snatched the water glass from beside the bed, stood looking around for a moment, and then strode over to the window. He drew back the curtain, hefted the sash and threw the water outside. A faint muffled noise suggested he had not looked below. I wondered who had got the unexpected wetting.

'Right,' he said, and came back and scooped some water out of the bucket. 'I'll run along and see to this while you finish checking the room. I imagine that man will have what I need in his rooms.'

'Do you have the key?'

He patted his waistcoat pocket. 'Always keep it on me!' he said and hurried out of the door carrying his glass of water aloft. Left alone, I pondered that either Fitzroy was play-acting for some reason, or the parts of his mind that thought he was Bertram were also accessing other parts that knew he was Fitzroy. I hoped this was good, but his recent actions, although probably harmless, seemed entirely nonsensical. I sighed heavily.

I went to the centre of the room, and it was dark outside, so the drawn curtains added no extra light. I closed my eyes and breathed deeply. Then I opened them and turned slowly on the spot in an attempt to see if anything was out of place, if there was anything off in Esmeralda's room. My conclusion was that despite her having a predilection for wearing men's socks, the room was normal. I had my hand on the door, and was about to leave, when the hairbrushes on her dressing table caught my attention.

Some women do have more than one brush. A strong one for detangling and another for adding shine. Esmeralda had three. My own hair had only recently grown back to shoulder-length. I still rather hated all the fuss that goes with long hair. Fitzroy had once, to Bertram's horror, cut it short, and freed me from the burden of caring for my waist-length hair. It had been a revelation, and if fashion and my husband had allowed, I would have always worn it very short. Still, three hairbrushes?

I went back across to the dressing table. I picked them up in turn. The first was the standard hard brush, the second the shine brush, but the third appeared to be minimally used. It also seemed to be a twin to the second. I twisted the back experimentally, and it came off in my hands. A piece of folded paper fluttered out.

I opened it up. I couldn't read a word, but I knew enough to know the script was entirely in German.

Chapter Thirty-six

Clues

I hurried to Fitzroy's rooms, only to find them locked and the sound of snoring coming from inside. I knocked hard, but there was no answer. I dashed down the stairs again and almost ran into Griffin. I explained my predicament.

'It's best to let him sleep,' said the major-domo. 'Why don't you take this to McLeod? It's most pertinent to his investigation, isn't it?'

I wasn't sure that was true, but I agreed. Rory did need to know. Unfortunately, it transpired he had also retired for the night, and so I once again found myself knocking on the door of a sleeping man. Rory, however, whether from police training or from once being a butler and thus having had to deal with unreasonable demands at a moment's notice, came to the door swiftly, wearing a dressing gown. The room behind him was in darkness. He pulled the door shut, scowling at me. 'Jane is asleep!'

'And Esmeralda had a German letter among her possessions, hidden in a hairbrush.'

He took the letter from me, still scowling. 'Have you had Hans translate it?'

I shook my head. 'I didn't think you would want that, as he is still a suspect.'

The scowl lifted a little. 'Thank you. I know you believe him innocent, but that was well considered.'

I tried to take this as a compliment, and not, as it felt, a pat on the head. 'Fitzroy reads German,' I said. 'But he appears to be fast asleep and Griffin thinks I should leave him alone.'

'No one else knows you have found this?' I shook my head. 'Well, in that case, I think we can leave it to the morning. I take it you brought it to me to keep in my custody?'

I nodded. 'It seemed most fitting,' I said.

'It strikes me that you are far more sensible and amendable when in your own home,' said Rory. 'Perhaps this escapade will convince you to abandon your mad adventures with Fitzroy – that is if he ever regains his mind. This version of you, Euphemia, is by far the most ladylike.'

As I liked Jane, I did not react in a manner to reduce the likelihood of Rory being able to father her children. I even held my temper. Goodness knows I needed Rory onside if there was not to be an almighty fuss back at the department when this was all over. So, I smiled, nodded and retired to my own chamber, where I found Bertram and several pillows, which I punched very hard. Then we talked long into the night.

Breakfast saw me hopeful that the situation was soon to be resolved. Fitzroy was already down and eating like a horse. He sat at the head of the table, and had his plate piled indecently high. Bertram had had to settle for a tray in our room and had been brought rather low by the meagre two eggs and bacon that he had been sent. Fitzroy, seated in my husband's rightful place, grinned at me delightedly as I entered the dining room. 'My love, come and sit by my side. I will serve you breakfast.' He pulled out a chair for me and then hurried to the buffet to fill a plate for me. I noticed he also took the opportunity to eat a couple of bacon slices with his bare fingers from the serving dish. He returned to the table wearing a boyish smile and licking his fingers. 'I don't know what's up with me today, but I'm damnably hungry!'

I noticed that he had indeed put everything I would have chosen for myself on my plate. Something my husband would have struggled to do. It gave me a very odd feeling. Fitzroy continued to beam at me in between shovelling food into his face. 'Did you sleep well, my dear? I had the oddest dreams. When we are alone I shall tell you about them!' he whispered in my ear.

'I found a hidden letter, after you left,' I said softly. 'Rory has it. You should take a look at it after breakfast.'

Fitzroy's eyes gleamed. 'Top-hole!' he said, saluting with his knife. Mrs Gruber, seated on our right, raised her hand to smother a smile. Rory, further down the table, raised his eyes to heaven. Alex frowned. I had never heard either Bertram or Fitzroy use such an expression and feared that this might be a third emergent personality. This quashed my appetite. However, Fitzroy kept jostling at me to eat, so I did as I was bid.

Afterwards I dragged him into the small library, where before I could protest, he gathered me into his arms and gave me a rather bacon-y kiss. How I might have dealt with the situation was rendered moot by the appearance of Rory, who had rightly surmised I would meet him here.

Fitzroy loosened his grip on me. 'Lovely way to start the day, don't you find, McLeod, kissing your wife?' He pulled a monocle out of his pocket and screwed it in. He peered at Rory. 'Not that your marital status has made you more amenable. You're still rather kipper-faced.'

I gently broke away from him. 'The letter,' I said, holding out my hand to Rory. He pulled it wordlessly from his inside pocket and handed it to me. I gave it to Fitzroy. He scanned the paper quickly. 'Hmmf,' he said, 'instructions to get close to Hans to see if he can be turned as an asset, and,' he flipped it over, 'a scribbled note by someone else on getting here and observing.' He shrugged and handed it back to Rory. 'Clearly, she was a German spy. How and if she succeeded with Hans we will have to enquire. What interests me is the note written in the second hand – it doesn't say if she is to observe only, or if she is . . . well, you know, meant to engage with the rest of us.'

'You mean attack?' said Rory.

'Good grief, no, man. It would be suicide to act offensively among so many foreign agents. I meant talk to us about the possibility of a peace!'

Rory held out his hand for the letter. Fitzroy rather pointedly handed it to me. 'Secrets of the realm, I think,' he said. 'Not for Mr Plod and co.'

Rory scowled. 'I didn't think you read German, Bertram,' he said.

Confusion flashed across Fitzroy's face. I put my hand on his arm. 'He has been learning of late,' I said. 'Couldn't quite manage a novel yet, could you, darling? But a few simple words of a note are not beyond him.'

Fitzroy patted my arm. His expression returned to normal. 'Well, you know, old chap, some of us try to keep the old brain ticking over.'

Rory made a growly sort of noise and banged out of the room.

'Such a rude fellow,' said Fitzroy. 'What do you make of all this?'

'Apart from the obvious?' I said. 'We shall have to interrogate Hans.'

Fitzroy nodded. 'Is that going to be difficult for you?'

I shook my head. 'What is difficult for me is knowing what you were up to with that sock last night!'

Fitzroy laughed. 'Thought I'd lost my marbles, did you?'

'Frankly, yes.'

'There was this chappie caught the other day who had smuggled invisible ink in his socks. He only needed to add water and he could extract the ink and write his secret notes. One of theirs – a spy, but not a very good one. So, when I saw a lady's luggage with men's socks, I naturally wondered.'

'Naturally,' I said, sinking into a seat. 'So, you were distilling it and trying it out. I take it it needed a re-agent?'

'Yes, all the stuff was up in that man's room, but I felt a bit sleepy. Put my head down for a minute and it was lights out. I think he had the room booby-trapped somehow. Wretched fellow.'

'So, you don't know if the sock . . .'

'Hardly matters since you found the letter. Tell me all about that, while we go and root Hans out. He's not actually locked up, is he?'

Chapter Thirty-seven

Hans Muller

From the wary expression on Hans's face I surmised hopefully that someone had told him about Fitzroy's current mental state. Mrs T had moved Hans to a small suite, so he could stay sequestered away from the rest of the party, but he wasn't officially confined. We found him, sitting by his fireside in the small saloon, a discarded book at his feet, and an untouched plate of muffins on the small table beside him. Fitzroy and I remained standing in a show of undiscussed intimidation. Rather than explain, Fitzroy handed him the note. He also took the opportunity to steal a muffin.

Hans glanced at the paper. His expression changed and his attention sharpened as he read through it. 'She was a trap for me?' he said.

'I can't work out if she met us on the train by accident or as part of a plan,' I said.

'I imagine she had been briefed about him,' said Fitzroy, somewhat thickly through the remains of the muffin, 'but the meeting on the train on your way to Scotland was a happy accident for her.'

'That would explain why, once she had his attention, she clung like a limpet.'

'But I didn't even tell her my real name,' said Hans.

'Are you sure you didn't let it slip?' I asked.

Hans shook his head. 'As I said,' continued Fitzroy, 'I expect she had files on any foreign nationals who were related to members of government or agents of the Crown. If I was heading over to Germany, I'd brush up on potential assets before I left. Certainly the female ones.'

'So, she would have threatened to tell Richenda about our affair . . .' Hans dropped his head in his hands.

'That's the thing,' said Fitzroy. 'As I understand it you managed to make it very clear to Richenda what you were up to.' Hans gave a low moan. 'So you were no use to her anymore. I can imagine in the circumstances she would have tried to make a quick exit – but the snow forced her to wait around. Really, it makes your wife the most likely suspect.'

Hans looked up sharply. 'But the others, the other spies – she was a German spy!'

'There are many things they might have done,' said Fitzroy, 'but killing her was not one of them.'

Hans looked at me appealingly. 'Euphemia!'

I sat down on the edge of a chair facing him. 'I'm sorry, Hans, but he's right. She would either have been seen as a source of information or possibly as someone who could start a back-channel discussion on peace. She was far more valuable alive.'

'Oh God!' said Hans. 'It's all my fault.'

'Yes,' said Fitzroy. 'It is. I need to know if you would have considered turning.'

'My children are British citizens,' said Hans, 'so no. Never. I have no love of Germany as my parents did.'

'Your children could have been used as leverage,' said Fitzroy. He took a step closer to Hans's chair, looming over him, so Hans had to crook his neck to look up at him.

'I suppose so,' said Hans. 'But I know the way these things work. The only way to keep them safe would have been to disclose all to the British authorities. I realise they might have locked me up, as I hadn't been staying where I was meant to be – but I'd rather be under British protection or even in custody than be blackmailed.'

Fitzroy and I left him alone. 'Do you believe him?' I asked Fitzroy when we were outside.

'He's smart enough to know blackmail never ends well,' said Fitzroy. 'But then many victims do and still they cannot find another solution. I know he is fond of you, and I think he trusts you, so yes, I think he would have come to you if he had got himself into hot water.'

'Did you agree he could bring his mistress to this meeting?'

Fitzroy flushed slightly. 'He may have misinterpreted something I said.'

'I see,' I said, injecting as much cold as I could into my voice.

'Let's go into the little library,' said Fitzroy. 'I can hear a decanter calling my name. I need you to run through the people we have here again.'

'I thought you'd want to talk to Richenda?'

'It's not really my business if she killed the woman. My concern is with more . . . er—'

'Espionage-orientated facets of the situation?'

'Oh, well put!'

Chapter Thirty-eight

Where are the Germans Redux?

In the library, nursing a glass of whisky I didn't want, I ran through our guests once more, and who Alex and I believed they represented.

'Hmm,' said Fitzroy when I had finished. 'There's definitely three lots that strike me as odd.'

'Only three?'

'Yes, well, I grant you they're all a bit odd. But Alex knew the most details about the plan. I can't think why his Emperor would want him to sabotage it unless he's suddenly decided his future lies on the German side.' He held up his hand. 'Thing is, I reckon Alex might mess up when it came to a woman. He'd have a lot of trouble overcoming his gentlemanly scruples.'

'That can only possibly make sense if... no, I can't make it make sense at all,' I said, shaking my head.

'I can't either,' admitted Fitzroy. 'But he's still the one who knew the most about the plan – and well, he doesn't like killing women. It would upset him dreadfully.'

'He's shown no signs of distress while you were away.'

Fitzroy poured himself another drink. I held on firmly to my glass so he couldn't refill it. 'Yes, you're right as usual. But I can't help it. I have a feeling that something is off with him.'

'Are we discounting more outlandish notions like Hans or Richenda?'

'Humph,' said Fitzroy, throwing himself back down in his seat, and somehow not spilling as much as a drop. 'We both know that soldiers from the front line can . . . well . . . look at Willoughby.'

'I thought he was doing terribly well undercover.'

'From what you've said, he hasn't had another fit, but he's not exactly helped out, has he?' said Fitzroy, sipping his whisky. 'You don't think Rory could have lost control, do you?'

'And murdered Esmeralda? But he wasn't—'

Fitzroy cut me off. 'I can see you're shocked but the man has a detailed list of where everyone should have been according to your servants, and a list of where a lot of them actually were that morning. Yet he says he finds no help from this. I take it you looked at his tables, diagrams, whatevers?'

'No,' I said slowly, 'and he hasn't offered to show me. Are you thinking if he realised Esmeralda was German he might have committed some kind of revenge killing?'

'I'm suggesting it as a possibility. You know him better than I do.'

I looked into my heart, and although I found it unlikely, I discovered I couldn't rule it out. It had after all been easy to persuade him to come here, and he had arrived very quickly despite the weather. Almost magically fast. Had he been hiding nearby? But what of Jane? Too devoted to ask questions? Fitzroy was still speaking.

'Charlie interests me too,' he said. 'My guess is he's an industrialist of some sort who had the connections to hear about this. His only motivation is likely to be making money out of the war, so . . .'

'He wouldn't want to end it?' I found that my voice rose alarmingly at the end of this sentence.

'My dear girl, I'm only offering an outside perspective. View from the crow's nest. Which reminds me, those chaps pretending to be army? I'm pretty certain they're Naval Intelligence trying to get an inside look. Never have trusted those chappies.'

'Why?' I felt as if I had been the one swallowing the whisky.

'My father was involved in all that malarkey. Wouldn't have trusted that man with the key to an outhouse. Shifty types in that department. It's been around a few centuries and instead of realising how old-fashioned they are, they think they're the bee's knees whenever a war turns up. Insufferable toads, the lot of them.'

'But you like sailing,' I said. 'You've been talking about getting your own yacht.'

'Have I, my God,' said Fitzroy. 'You want to stamp on that idea. Bertram at sea doesn't bear thinking about.'

'Bertram?' I queried.

Fitzroy shot out of his seat. 'Me, I mean me.' He poured a third whisky and then saw my expression. 'Last one, wife, then we can set off. Lots of the others are dubious, but what else can you expect?'

'So, Alex, Rory and Charlie?'

'Got you calling him Alex, has he? I don't like that. He's as bad a womaniser as that man. You had better watch yourself around him.'

'As you well know I am more than able to take care of myself,' I said, standing.

'Never wise to discount the abilities of operatives who have been in the field longer than you, Alice. I mean, the man's a friend of mine and I wouldn't turn my back on him.'

'Of yours or of Fitzroy's?' I pressed.

Fitzroy threw back the rest of his drink. 'Oh, stop chattering, woman. We have to pop by Richenda and Hans too.' He looked at me hard. 'Obviously?'

I had no idea, but I nodded.

'I suppose for the sake of rigorousness we should include Mimi and What's-her-face. Can't see them doing it though.'

'Women can't be assassins?'

'Course they can be! Bloody good ones too. But I can't see the connection. Pretty sure they're Russian. Allies and all that. If there was a problem it would only be good manners to come to the host. We're on the same side. And besides, they are terribly frail. Easily overcome by a fit, young woman like Esmeralda, I would have thought. Still, wish I knew which faction they favoured.' He shook his head. 'Not that I suppose it matters much.'

Whatever had affected his sense of self, Fitzroy seemed both fit of body as he loped up the stairs, and more than aware of his surroundings. He knocked on Hans's door and, without waiting for an answer, stuck his head in. I didn't hear what he said as he closed the door quickly again, and said merely, 'That should do it. Richenda still in the tower?'

He didn't wait for me to answer before setting a rapid pace in that direction. As I was wearing a morning dress, my movement was hampered, and I again arrived behind, panting heavily. This time the door was open, and I could see Richenda sitting in a chair, sobbing. My sister-in-law is not a quiet crier, so I was not entirely surprised when Fitzroy shut the door on her. He turned and saw me. 'Do keep up, Alice,' he said. 'You're missing all the good bits.'

'What – you can't – let me past.'

Fitzroy caught me by the elbows and prevented me from passing. 'I've just been playing matchmaker. I've told them both the other is liable to be hanged for the murder. If that doesn't mend things between them, I don't know what will. You never want something as much as when you know you've lost it.' He kissed me on the forehead. 'Now, let's find Rory. Wasn't in the library, so he must have set himself up a little office somewhere else. Possibly below stairs. That's his natural habitat. Somewhere dark and grim. Like a mushroom. Let's beard Giles in his den. He'll know where and possibly more.' He released me and set off at breakneck speed towards the servants' stairs. Of course, he knew where all the servants' passageways in the house were, I told myself as I trotted as fast as I could down the wooden stairs behind him.

Chapter Thirty-nine

Giles is Incommoded

'What ho, Giles!'

Fitzroy barged into our butler's pantry. Giles, who had been sitting at a small table with the epergne in pieces in front of him, shot to his feet.

I took a moment to orientate myself. I never intruded into what I felt was the private life of my servants. I knew, of course, the layout of the pantry. It was a dark panelled room of some spaciousness. There was enough room for Giles and Mrs T to have a quiet cup of tea together and discuss matters of the day. One section of wall had the very best china secured behind glass, and behind one panel lay our safe with all the other silverware and such stuff. Off to the left was a short staircase down to the even lower wine cellar that we had only recently succeeded in making waterproof. Giles's personal rooms, a further living space and a bedroom, were next door. Bertram had once remarked it was as if we were giving the man his own flat. But really a good butler is more than worth it. That is, if Giles chose to stay with us after this intrusion.

'Sir! I wasn't expecting . . .' Giles scraped back his chair, and stood there staring, cloth in one hand and polish in the other. I had never seen him look so undignified, and I felt for him.

'Don't worry, old chap.' Fitzroy wandered into the room and picked up a piece of the epergne, a rather over-stylised palm tree with attached pineapples and elephants at the foot. 'It is totally ghastly, isn't it?' he said.

'It's a Stapleford heirloom, sir,' said Giles stiffly.

'It's ugly and it makes it hard to talk to people,' said Fitzroy bluntly. 'Do you like it, wife?'

'Not particularly,' I said.

'Good,' said Fitzroy, 'throw it out. There's a good butler. You can spend your time on better things.'

My butler inflated with indignation before my eyes. I slid back slightly out of Fitzroy's peripheral vision, and shook my head at the wide-eyed Giles, who let out a deep breath of relief. He returned to a less imposing posture. 'Can I help you, sir?'

'Hmm, what?' Fitzroy seemed fascinated by the room and the treasures on display. 'Oh yes, what room is McLeod using for his musing?'

'The music room, sir.'

'Never have guessed that,' said Fitzroy and with a rude abruptness he turned and left.

'I'm so sorry,' I said. 'He's really not himself.'

'I understood that to be the case from Mr Griffin. I had not however realised how, er, excitable he would be. Would you like me to fetch help, madam? I worry for your safety.'

'Whatever else Fitzroy may do, or break, he won't hurt me,' I said.

'If you say so, ma'am.'

'He thinks he is my husband,' I said, 'and Bertram loves me.'

'Very good, madam,' said my poor butler, blushing to the tips of his ears. I took pity on him and left without further explanation. Really, I needed to get to the music room as soon as possible. It was not beyond the bounds of possibility that Fitzroy would decide that it was all Rory's fault and try to strangle a confession out of him. He had come to loathe him, when Rory and I were engaged. In fact, one of the only things Bertram and Fitzroy might agree on was their dislike of McLeod. I lifted the hem of my skirts and fairly ran down the passageway after him.

I am ashamed to say we rarely used the music room. The damp in the Fens air played the devil with any instrument, but also I was not a lover of making music. Of course, my mother had ensured I could play, and Bertram had once told me of his childish misadventures with an oboe, but between us we were not a musical pair.

The music room with its plaster ornaments of white and blue, a little like a Wedgwood bowl, had not yet been renovated. It was a square room that sat at the end of one of the wings, with large windows facing out on to the wild Fen landscape, which sounds lovely, but made it exceedingly cold. The curtains needed replacing and the carpet was threadbare. I hadn't ordered the room to be lit for some weeks. In fact, I had thought it locked and out of bounds to guests.

I entered the room to hear Fitzroy say, 'So this is where you have hidden yourself away! Not very sporting of you, is it?'

As I stepped into the room, I felt ashamed that any guest should see it, and a shiver of cold passed through me. Rory had convinced someone to light a fire in the white marble fireplace, but weeks of chill are not easily lifted from a room. He could have burnt an entire oak, and it would not have made much difference.

My teeth must have chattered, as Fitzroy turned and drew me against him with one arm. 'See what you've done now, man! You've made my wife cold!'

Rory stood beside a small round table, which he had covered with papers. More of these spread out over the top of the long-forsaken white grand piano. I say white, but it looked more like grey. There was a great deal of dust in the room, and I could feel it tickling the inside of my nose.

'I take it he is still under the delusion—'

'Yes,' I said quickly. 'Hans does think the murder was committed by Richenda.'

'Bring your papers and your charts, and we can retire to the warmth of the library. I need to see your notes.'

Fitzroy released me and set off as quickly as he had entered. 'This cannot carry on,' said Rory. 'He is clearly mad and needs to be locked up.'

'I disagree. He is in an excitable state, but he has some interesting ideas about the situation.'

Rory scowled at me. 'He is manhandling you.'

Many retorts rose to my lips, but I merely said, 'Bertram is fully advised of the situation, and his is the only opinion that should and does matter to me.'

I moved to the piano to start gathering the papers. 'Not like that!' cried Rory. 'There is an order.'

'Then you had better do it,' I said. And I waited until he had.

Chapter Forty

The Spy is Unmasked

I had once loved my library, but I was in growing danger of coming to hate it. 'Here we are again,' said Fitzroy merrily as we settled in front of a large table. He brought a couple of lamps across and turned the gas up full. 'Now then, what have you got, McLeod? Anything at all?'

'Wait,' I said, 'we need to confirm with Rory that Esmeralda was a German spy. It seems likely she was killed because of this either by someone with a hatred of Germany, or someone who did not want the peace discussions to have any success.'

Rory nodded. 'That does clarify things a little – although in my experience the most likely motives for killing are the simple ones. Even in your world.'

'Such as jealousy,' I said.

Fitzroy, who had been fidgeting impatiently, leaned forward and grabbed one of Rory's papers. 'Have you managed to rule yourself out, McLeod?'

Rory, who had put forward a hand to retrieve the paper, fell back in his chair. 'I didn't arrive until afterwards,' he said.

'The best alibi,' said Fitzroy. 'Used it myself more than once.'

'Fitzroy—Bertram,' I corrected myself, but not before Fitzroy gave me an odd look. 'You know how your constitution is frail—'

'Nonsense. I'm as fit as an ox.'

'I mean your heart, my dear.'

'Ah, yes,' said Fitzroy, and again I saw the puzzlement in his eyes. 'You have been getting too excited. I think you need a rest. Why not use those rooms where you were last night. Out of the way for some peace and quiet. I will send tea to your room in an hour or two when you are rested.'

I thought he would protest, but Fitzroy shook his head from side to side like an old lion being bothered by flies, and not quite strong enough to frighten them away. 'You may be right,' he said. 'My head is beginning to ache.'

I took his arm and helped him stand. There was so much confusion on his face that I had the oddest impulse to hug him, something I never do, but I restrained myself. I patted him on the arm and told him to sleep well.

The door closed behind him. 'You seem quite immersed in the role of playing his doting wife,' said Rory.

'I am concerned for him,' I said. 'He is a dear and good friend.'

'There is nothing good about that man,' said Rory, half under his breath. He reached forward and rearranged the papers more to his liking. 'Bearing in mind what you have told me, if it does have any bearing on the event, that is . . .'

'If she was murdered for being a spy,' I said.

'Yes,' said Rory looking directly at me. 'If she was murdered for being part of that nasty world of yours, we need to know if Hans Muller had realised she was a spy, and if he had voiced that suspicion to anyone.'

'I don't believe he would have killed her for that. I rather think he would have come running to me.'

Rory's upper lip curled unpleasantly. 'He was always fond of you.'

'Because he is my asset,' I said icily. 'He was working for me when she latched on to us. I got London to check to see if there was anything on her then and they came up with nothing. Which suggests she was either new to the game, or high-ranking enough—' I broke off as realisation dawned. 'That's what she meant. Oh, what a fool I have been. She told me she was a spy when she was dying. She was trying to tell me it was why she was killed. And I thought she was talking about parlour games! Poor woman, she had lost so much blood, and she must have been trying so hard to make me understand . . .'

'I don't understand the half of that, but I take from it that you now believe Esmeralda wanted you to know she was a spy and that was why she was killed?'

'Yes.'

'She said nothing else?'

I shook my head. 'I could see by her eyes there was little life left to her. When she said, "It was a good game," it cost her a great effort. I think now it was only a part of what she wanted to say. I think she wanted to tell me who had killed her, but it was important, for some reason, that I first understood she was a spy.'

'As you say, thoughts become confused on the verge of demise. A pity though. We might have been spared all this.' He gestured at the papers before him. 'I shall have to consider how this new evidence moves things forward.'

'I am happy to offer my help if you want to sound out ideas or might want me to interview people?'

Rory gave me a long look. I returned it quite unabashed. Eventually he said, 'I think not.'

I smiled and rose. 'Good luck then,' I said, and left. I perversely hoped my refusal to argue with him had annoyed him. I went and found the real Bertram and told him what had been happening.

Chapter Forty-one

A Lack of Facts

'Yes, well, Rory McLeod has always seemed an odd sort of chap to me,' said Bertram. 'Controlling type. Can be dashedly unpleasant. Big chip on his shoulder over being a servant – not that anyone made him do it.'

'He was a rather good butler,' I said.

'Making order out of chaos,' said Bertram, who was sitting in his dressing room that lay alongside our bedroom. He'd made a sort of nest for himself with decanters, a plate of sandwiches, a selection of his favourite novels and the day's papers. He had a notebook open on a side table. He reclined under a tartan blanket on a red chaise longue I had bought him. I sat on a corner chair. 'Want this?' he said, indicating his seat.

I shook my head. 'You've been robbed of your persona for the day. The least I can do is leave you your comforts.'

My husband grinned sheepishly at me. 'I've got a hot pig under here,' he said, referring to the old stone water bottles he preferred. 'How much longer, do you think?'

'Oh, bits of the old Fitzroy are already coming back – snippets of language and the like.' I added the last part quickly. 'I wouldn't be surprised if he woke up knowing who he was.'

'Euphemia,' said Bertram awkwardly, 'Euphemia . . .'

'Have I considered he might be the killer?' I said. 'Yes, I have. I can even see that hating to harm a woman might have caused him to botch it. But I can't imagine he would leave her to die slowly, and above all I can't think of why.'

'Something from his nefarious past?' suggested Bertram, twisting the corners of his blanket, so he didn't have to look me in the eye.

'I genuinely think he would have told me. I don't mean necessarily told me about the past, but he would have told me we had a problem with Esmeralda. According to Hans, Fitzroy seems to have encouraged him to bring her.' I bit my lip. 'But then he might not have known who she was, or he might have known that I checked up on her with the department. Not that I could give them more than her first name, the story she told and a description.' I exhaled in frustration. 'It is no use. This sends me round in circles again. I don't think he would have left anyone in that state.'

'What if he had some kind of brainstorm?' asked Bertram.

'Oh, do leave that fringe alone,' I said. 'You'll unravel the whole thing. You didn't worry about asking me if it might be Fitzroy. Of course I considered him, and I have no particular reason to suspect him – and some good reasons not to. But when we come to brainstorms, and people not knowing their actions, why even I might have done it!'

Bertram released the fringe. 'I see your point. We need facts.'

'I'm damned if I know how we can uncover any more,' I said. I saw the look on his face. 'Sorry,' I said. 'I don't often swear, but this puzzle is as bad a tangle as I have ever come across.'

'It does seem that way,' said Bertram. 'Who would benefit from killing her?'

'Other than Richenda despatching a jealous rival? Someone who didn't want her at the meeting. But we need to know if that was because she was for or against the war.'

'Who would be for the war!' asked Bertram.

'Fitzroy thinks that chap Charlie might be an arms dealer,' I offered.

Bertram scowled heavily. 'Yes, that would do it.'

'I'm going to talk to him after luncheon. Shall I get Mrs Warburton to send you up a tray?'

'I have already given my instructions,' said Bertram, winking at me. Then he grew solemn. 'I say, Euphemia, we will have this lot out of the house before the festivities begin, shan't we?'

'I thought we might ask Hans and Richenda to stay. The weather looks likely to clear and they can send for their children.'

'That would be rather jolly. I suppose you want that man to stay on too?'

'It's either that or send him off to his father, who hates him.'

'No, I wouldn't do that,' said Bertram. 'I know that feeling all too well. I might not like the man much, but I'd spare him that.' He grinned at me. 'But then he might always end up in an asylum.'

I threw a cushion at my husband, who immediately used it as extra lumbar support. I went off to find luncheon and then Charlie. My mind still went in circles. There must be something that I was missing. Some thread that if I tugged on it would unfurl the whole dratted puzzle.

Luncheon had once more become a buffet with the dining room filled with smaller tables. It struck me as a lot of work for the staff to take out all the leaves of the big table, remove it and then bring in the separate smaller tables. I wasn't even sure whose idea it had been to do this. I suspected von Nacht. Smaller tables encouraged more intimate conversation. Indeed, my eyes had scarcely run along the trestle tables with the selection of various dishes when I spotted Hans and Richenda sitting together. I would not have described them as billing and cooing, but the fact they were dining *à deux*, and no one was crying or shouting, was a big step forward.

'Told you,' said Fitzroy's voice in my ear.

I must have jumped several inches in the air, but at least I managed to suppress the squeak that built in my chest.

'I thought you were lying down, husband.'

'Short nap. Never could manage to sleep a long time. Seems such a waste. And yes, delightful though it would be to continue the charade, I am now fully aware of who I am.'

'You feel well?' I asked. The red flush had gone from his face, and his eyes no longer shone in that overexcited manner.

'Tip-top,' he said. 'But I am enormously hungry. Let's gather the vitals and have a chinwag.'

This sounded like the original and one and only Fitzroy. Unaccountably, I felt tears sting my eyes. I dashed them away with the back of my hand. 'Buck up, old girl,' said Fitzroy. 'You're not going to get rid of me that easily.'

'There was talk of putting you in an asylum!' I said.

Fitzroy handed me a plate and took one for himself. He started loading first my plate and then his. 'Yes, well, I suppose I do know a lot of stuff. I bet McLeod and Giles were all in favour.' He gave a small chuckle. 'It will be my pleasure to disappoint them. Ooh, look, ham, wafer-thin too.'

'I don't know how we will have anything left for Christmas if this lot doesn't leave soon,' I said.

'I thought of that when I awoke. One of your excellent young fellows is winging his way to the post office to send up some supplies I have. Not just the quaffable type. I should be able to contribute a few joints and at least some spuds.'

'How?'

Fitzroy tapped the side of his nose. 'Let's eat, and then we need to gather a few characters together and unleash my plan!'

We walked to a table. Then before he sat down, Fitzroy loudly announced, 'In case anyone was concerned for my health, I am happy to report I am once more in possession of all my faculties, and know exactly who I am.' He then sat down to eat. To my surprise, but not his, the room applauded him. Of course they did. He rose once more and acknowledged them like a king nodding to his subjects. I resisted the temptation to stick my fork in his arm.

Chapter Forty-two

Fitzroy Reveals His Plan

When we had finished eating, Fitzroy had signalled to some tables, caught the attention of some maids to carry messages and without leaving his seat arranged for his chosen party to meet him in the library. We were Griffin, Willoughby, Giles, McLeod, Bertram and myself.

He gestured to us all to be seated. Giles stood awkwardly at the back. Fitzroy pointed at him and at a seat, much in the way he would command Jack. Giles sat. Standing in front of the hearth, Fitzroy addressed us all. 'We have been going about this all wrong. Each of you is present because you are without question not guilty of the attack that took Esmeralda's life, and therefore vital to my plan.'

'Are you sure you're up to this, old chap?' asked Bertram. 'Not that I'm not glad to have my name and my wife back!'

Fitzroy waved his hand dismissively at this. 'I thank you for your concern, but we must push on and get this thing done.'

'That is exactly what I have been trying to do,' said Rory acerbically.

'And if you don't mind me saying so, with very little success,' said Fitzroy. Rory tried to interject, but Fitzroy spoke over him. 'The problem is you have all been going about this the wrong way. There are simply not enough facts to draw a conclusion.'

'Well, that's it then,' said Rory. 'We might as well all go home.'

Fitzroy regarded him from his superior height. Both were tall men and there was less than two inches between them, but somehow

Fitzroy pulled it off. 'I must say, old man, you seem to have a bit of a bad attitude here. I realise the whole thing has come as a nasty shock with you meant to be on your honeymoon, but there is no need to be so confrontational.'

'Me! My attitude!' said Rory. He threw up his hands. 'Oh, I give up.'

'No, no. Never fear, I have the solution,' said Fitzroy. 'All this must have been terribly trying for you. No one doubts your tenacity and bravery, but . . .' I could practically see the steam boiling under Rory's collar. Fortunately, before Fitzroy could belittle him any more, there was a knock on the door and Archie came in. His hair was plastered to his head in a vain attempt to look respectable, and his collar was at all angles. A faint odour of the stables followed him. Fitzroy gestured to the young man and then beckoned him in. 'This is young Archie, who so staunchly kept my secret when I went out on a horse. He's a grand little chap, Stapleford, and if you don't do something for him, I reckon I will. Anyway, he is vital to my plan.'

'Eric,' I said, using his real name. 'Do you think you could possibly tell us what this plan of yours is.'

'Right! Right! Burning daylight and all that. We need to set a trap!'

There was immediately an outbreak of voices and a great deal of consternation. Fitzroy let us all twitter on for a while and took the opportunity to pour himself a whisky.

'Should he be drinking that much?' I whispered to Griffin. 'Is he really himself?'

'Oh yes. He's Fitzroy all right. Crazy madcap schemes. He'll be drinking whisky to dull the headache. When he went to lie down he had a severe migraine. Anyone else wouldn't be on their feet right now. Anyway, the brainstorm appears to all intents and purposes to have brought him back to himself. Unless, of course, this new plan involves flying pigs.'

'Now listen!' said Fitzroy, raising his voice above the noise. 'Young Archie is going to be promoted to junior footman for the evening. His main job will be to set the red wine glasses on the table, and when he is collecting them ensure that he knows whose was whose. Obviously, there is a table plan for dinner, drawn up by the competent Mr Giles, but I want Archie to collect these glasses one by one, so he can place them in separate areas of the tray.'

'What the devil for?' asked Bertram.

'Because I shall take them away and examine them for fingerprints. These I shall compare to the fingerprints on the weapon.'

'Good grief! That's so damn simple,' said Bertram. 'Why didn't you think of that, McLeod?'

'Leaving aside the not inconsiderable difficulty of collecting the prints of everyone in the house – I have no legal way to enforce cooperation of the foreign nationals. They have diplomatic immunity. We were unable to recover clear prints from the weapon.'

'I hope you haven't told anyone that,' said Fitzroy. 'Although I suppose I could claim a superior expertise.'

Bertram was frowning. I spoke up before he could. 'So, it is a ruse. You hope that the killer will believe you are able to discover their identity and attempt to silence you.'

'Pretty much,' said Fitzroy. 'We will have to ensure no one goes after McLeod, but I am more than happy to be the main target. I thought I would set up my fingerprinting laboratory in the music room. Although I would be grateful if we could build up the fire in there. It's cool as a tomb.' He winked at me, and whispered, 'Philistine.'

'Why, you could even play a little piano while you waited for the intruder,' said Bertram.

'Well, I'll have Alice to back me up. You'll notice I haven't included Alexander von Nacht in this discussion. I wanted to leave the field as wide as possible. I don't think he is the killer, but then there are both so many reasons to kill Esmeralda and not to kill her, and few of them fit together.'

'You can't put Euphemia in danger like that,' exclaimed Bertram.

I pulled him to one side as Fitzroy continued on with his plan. 'My dear,' I said quietly, 'what exactly do you think I do on missions? I can assure you it's not making the soup!'

'No,' said Fitzroy, overhearing us, 'she's a terrible cook.'

I gave him a filthy look, but he only grinned.

'So now we come to the heart of the thing. We need to let people know I am doing this without actually telling them. I have a few suggestions.'

'I am not at all surprised,' muttered Rory.

'McLeod, your role is merely to look hostile and disapproving at me. I think we could also stage a brief argument on a landing somewhere when I ask you for the murder weapon.'

'I can't give you that! It's evidence,' said Rory.

'You have to admit,' said Bertram, 'it's currently rather useless evidence.'

Rory muttered something that sounded decidedly hostile.

'Magnificent! You're well into the role already. Bertram, old chap, can you similarly make a bit of a fuss about how I'm still off my head. Only if you're really pushed do you give up the fingerprinting scheme. Hopefully someone will push you that far. Gruber, I imagine. He's the bullying sort.

'Archie will be making a careful round of picking up the red wine glasses before the dessert wine comes out. That should look terribly suspicious.'

Archie swallowed hard and looked at his feet. Fitzroy clapped him on the shoulder. 'Don't worry, lad. It doesn't matter if you make a mistake. It just has to look good. As Mrs Stapleford said, it's all a big trick.

'Now, Giles, if you could moan about me taking my protégé from the stables and introducing him into the dining room?'

Giles bowed slightly. 'I will have no difficulty in doing thus.'

'Griffin, you can be a kind of floating actor. You can drop a word here or there as you see fit to keep things going. Does that all make sense? Willoughby, I'm going to leave you to your own devices. You've been trained for this sort of thing – and your trainer is one of the best.' He smirked at this, so we clearly understood he meant himself.

'And I?'

'I rather presumed that you would avoid speaking badly of your partner behind his back.'

I nodded. 'But I think I would be worried if this was a real plan. So, I shall be distant and frowning.'

'Excellent,' said Fitzroy.

'This all assumes the assassin's skills are inferior to yours,' said Rory.

'Yes, what of it? Besides, there will be two of us – and I suppose the rest of you could hang around downstairs until the balloon goes up. No lurking in the hallways and giving our nefarious fly any reason not to step into my parlour.'

Chapter Forty-three

Curtains

I don't believe anyone was especially delighted at Fitzroy's plan. But as we dispersed, I felt as if the atmosphere had lightened a little. Giles was walking with the jauntiest step I had ever seen. Which admittedly was not that jaunty but indicated to anyone who knew him that he was rather proud of being included. Little Archie was gazing up at Fitzroy with the wide eyes of adoration, and also fairly bursting at the seams with pride. Bertram had a wicked look on his face that I suspected meant he was looking forward to having permission to openly denigrate Fitzroy. As one who had once worked closely with him, I knew that even Rory, who outwardly showed little change, was excited. Whatever were to happen I imagine Rory hoped it would shift us from the doldrums we were in – and if Fitzroy was injured in the fallout then he didn't much mind. I was the only one who worried for Fitzroy's safety. His performance as he outlined his plan, obnoxious and overbearing, was a show he put on when he didn't want to spend time interacting with others, and wanted to get on with the job. However, in this case I feared he might also have been husbanding his energy.

The migraine would have affected, and might still be affecting, his vision, and the amount of whisky he was downing meant he was still in considerable pain. I wasn't concerned he might be inebriated. On more than one occasion I had seen him operate immaculately while under the influence of considerably more than he had drunk today. No, I was worried he remained too unwell.

I managed to take Griffin aside in the hallway and voice my concerns.

He sighed. 'If anything will make Fitzroy feel better it's getting into trouble. Don't worry, Euphemia, the man is as tough as old boots.'

'Where's Jack?' I asked.

'Being kept in Fitzroy's bedroom. You'll need to have the door repainted, I'm afraid. Fitzroy doesn't want him getting underfoot or distracting people.'

'Poor little thing.'

'Hmmf, that dog has had more steak and sausages than I have since we arrived.'

I smiled. 'It's a good sign he's looking after Jack.'

'Hardly,' said Griffin. 'If there was only one place left on a lifeboat, neither you nor I would get it. Fitzroy would give it to that ruddy dog.' He walked off, head down and frowning. Exactly how my partner wanted him.

I took a rather roundabout way to the music room, only to find Fitzroy was already there, and busy getting out his equipment: lens, powder brushes, strong light, drawing paper and pens. I noticed a faint trace of powder along the top of the piano.

'Tried to set up there,' said Fitzroy, noticing me. 'Surprisingly it's not level.'

'What kind of powder is it?'

'Oh, just powder,' said Fitzroy. He straightened and turned away from the lens he was fiddling with. 'Actually, it's face powder from Esmeralda's room.'

'Eric!'

'Would you rather I had taken it from your room?'

'I hardly ever wear the stuff,' I said. 'Spying and cosmetics don't work that well together.'

Fitzroy smirked. 'Not your kind of spying, anyway.'

'It seems disrespectful,' I said.

'She's dead. I find the whole idea of being respectful or disrespectful to someone who is no longer alive ridiculous.' He sighed. 'But think of it this way. It's helping to catch her killer.'

'What's to stop someone from coming in here and sabotaging it while we are all at dinner?'

Fitzroy ticked the points off on his fingers. 'Well, hopefully we'd notice someone leaving. Secondly, they'd likely get themselves covered in powder, or cut by broken glass. And finally, and most to the point, Willoughby will be stationed outside ready to tackle anyone who tries. He doesn't like witnessing violence, but I can assure you he is more than capable of committing it.'

I nodded. 'You seem to have covered all the bases. Now, let's just hope that everyone else has obeyed your instructions efficiently.'

It may have been my imagination, but when we did convene for dinner, there seemed to be a more animated atmosphere about the group. We had pre-dinner drinks in the library. The fire burned brightly. The curtains were closed against the night. There was something almost festive about the atmosphere. I hoped this meant the rumours had been well circulated, and everyone was anticipating an end to this charade. I no longer had much hope for the peace process here. I wanted these people out of my house, and I suspected that they too wished to be gone.

Richenda and Hans stood at the back of the room. They were talking quietly to one another, their faces reflecting seriousness in an almost mirror-like manner. However, neither of them was pulling away from the other, and their body language suggested they were comfortable being close. I went over to them.

'Good evening,' I said. 'It is good to see you talking. I wonder if now might be the right time to invite you to stay with us over Christmas. The children too, of course.'

Hans looked at his wife. Richenda gave me a small smile. 'Providing neither of us is arrested for murder, I think it might suit us very well. But I will need to think a little more and discuss things with Hans. We have been re-evaluating and renegotiating our relationship.'

Hans turned beetroot at this. 'How very modern,' I said in an unnaturally bright voice. 'Of course you must discuss matters. However, know that you are both most welcome.'

'Thank you, Euphemia,' said Hans in a slightly choked voice. 'We will bore you no longer with our affairs.' He looked reproachfully at his wife. Then realising his choice of words he turned an even deeper shade of crimson, so much so that I feared for his health. I made a quick escape and almost ran straight into Alex and Fitzroy.

'So, you're really back, old bean,' said Alex. 'This is tremendously topping.'

'You shouldn't try so hard to be British,' said Fitzroy with a distinct lack of charm. 'You sound ridiculous.'

'Why didn't you both involve me in your little scheme?' asked Alex.

'Because we don't know if you did it,' said Fitzroy bluntly and walked away.

Alex opened his eyes wide in shock. 'Is that true, Euphemia?'

'I think he doesn't want to talk about it openly,' I said. 'In fact, I fear I must pretend I do not know which scheme you refer to.' I winked at him. Alex's jaw dropped slightly. 'I didn't think you were the winking type,' he said. 'I find myself quite delighted.'

This was my cue to make a quick escape and take the arm of my husband. It was a breach of protocol for me to walk into dinner with him, but I felt that Bertram had put up with an awful lot and more than deserved my undivided attention. Until Fitzroy was in the process of working in his makeshift laboratory, there was little for me to do.

Dinner began with a most excellent beetroot soup. This is of course a highly dangerous commodity for ladies dressed in evening wear, so the conversation was muted until the course was removed and the dangers of unwanted staining over. My own gown was a shining white, and I noticed that most of the ladies had chosen pale and light hues. The snow outside must be working on our imaginations.

The following courses, which came thick and fast, were in contrast somewhat lacklustre in colouring. As long as the food tastes good, and is reasonably presented, I don't normally note such things. Perhaps I was simply too tired of opening my curtains of a morning and seeing snow. Ice-cold, smothering snow, that kept all things uncomfortably static.

'I think I shall wear crimson to Christmas dinner,' I said suddenly to Bertram. 'I shall get my woman to run me up something suitable.'

'You will look lovely,' said my husband. 'A veritable queen of winter.'

Archie entered, dressed in a footman's suit that did not fit him, and which from his awkward gait he clearly did not find comfortable. I saw with growing fear his inability to lift his arms out from his side. He began to collect the glasses. He did this one by one and put them carefully on the tray that was placed on the sideboard in such a way that the top of it with carefully written name labels could not be seen.

'This isn't a precursor to you asking me to play Santa Claus to the Mullers' children, is it?' asked Bertram, suddenly suspicious.

'Oh, Fitzroy can do that,' I said without thinking, as my eyes continued to follow Archie. 'He'll love it.'

Bertram set down his knife. 'Wait a moment. A man has the right to play Santa Claus in his own house.'

Archie reached over and retrieved my glass. I detected only the slightest whiff of the stables, but it was clear he was much restricted by his uniform. I saw as he leaned across that his neck was red-raw in places where he must have been scratching. After he'd taken his glass, Bertram turned and whispered to me, 'Did you see that? I hope Fitzroy's ragamuffin hasn't brought in any little passengers from the stables. I shall order a hot bath tonight. I suggest you do the same.'

'I think his collar is too tight,' I whispered back.

'It's all too tight,' said Bertram. 'He looks like he might go pop at any moment. Let's hope he waits till he gets out of the dining room.' My husband chuckled at his little joke.

I watched nervously as Archie picked up the tray, and then, carrying it out ahead of him, as if it was some fearful creature that might attack at any moment, he made his way, with odd little steps, out of the room. I allowed myself to breathe once he had left. Fitzroy, at the other end of the table, caught my eye and winked. He was enjoying himself enormously. The fact Lucy was sitting next to him, wearing a scandalously low-cut dress, clearly had nothing to do with the matter. Honestly, the man was impossible!

Then came the sound of a loud crash. Fitzroy, who had gone back to looking down at Lucy from his superior height, and thus down the front of her décolletage, jerked his head up, and sent me a frantic message with his eyes.

'Excuse me, ladies and gentlemen,' I said, rising. 'I must ensure no one is hurt.'

I hurried out and across to the chamber where the kitchen brought things to await serving. I found Archie crying and Giles scolding him. The tray and the glasses were on the floor in bits.

'Sssh,' I said. 'Do not serve the trifle. I shall tell them it was that and the bowls that were smashed.'

'The stupid boy,' began Giles.

I shook my head. 'Not now. You can scold him later – although you might bear in mind that Archie was asked to do something for which he has not been trained.'

I hurried back to the dining room. 'Ladies and gentlemen,' I said, standing in the doorway. 'I fear I must tell you there has been another fatality. This time it was the trifle.'

'Poison,' squeaked Richenda.

'No, a foolish servant has dropped the pudding tray.'

There was a collective out-breath and then someone laughed. The laughter spread around the room, and the mood became so jolly that when only a cheese board was proffered, no one seemed to mind in the least.

Chapter Forty-four

The Trap is Readied

I had asked Jane to act as hostess for me once more. I could explain to her, as she was beyond suspicion, what was occurring. She was flattered by my trust. It seemed Rory had told her nothing. I resolved when this was all over to talk to her lady to lady about the handling of difficult gentlemen.

However, for now, her merry voice stole the room's attention as I slipped away to my station to support Fitzroy. Willoughby stood outside. 'No sign of anyone?' I whispered to him. He shook his head. 'Then I'll nip in and get behind the curtain,' I said.

'Watch your shoes,' he whispered to me.

'Go teach your granny,' I said rudely. 'Now, remove yourself from this location. You look too formidable as a guard.' He puffed out his chest a little at that, but made himself scarce.

Fitzroy gave me the slightest of nods as I moved as silently as I could across the room and took up my position. He was singing softly to himself as if he was completely absorbed in the glasses, fresh ones supplied by the kitchen, and the powder he was wielding with a free hand. He had removed his jacket and was working in his shirtsleeves. However, I noticed he had set up the lenses so that the reflections showed him the room behind him.

We waited. The curtains smelled musty and unpleasant. There was something beyond the mothballs sewn into the hem. I realised it was the slimy putrid scent of the Fens. As ever without constant vigilance the still, rotten water of the fields slunk into the house. It made me feel nauseous. Bertram never seemed to notice it.

It reminded me daily of death and decay. Oh, how I longed to live in London.

I attempted to pull my exposed skin away from the curtain fabric and bent my mind to the task at hand. I peeked through a slit in the curtains. Fitzroy was spreading around more powder. Eventually he began to draw on a sheet of paper, looking constantly from the glass to his page. Could he really accurately copy a fingermark, I wondered? Or was he passing the time drawing something else entirely? He had sung three separate songs in a low baritone before I heard the creak of a floorboard in the hallway. Only because I was watching him very closely did I see the momentary freeze of Fitzroy's movements. He didn't pause in his song or raise his voice.

'Oh hello,' said Mimi. 'I came to see what this was all about.' She moved further into the room. 'Of course we have heard of fingermarks back home, but can they really work in identifying a killer?' She peered bird-like with her neck stretched forward, a slender, almost too thin, ageing spinster in a dark lace gown. Drat it, I thought. How does one get rid of an inquisitive old lady? She reminded me of various ladies of my father's congregation who, without families or husbands of their own, hung around my father at church receptions asking almost impenetrable questions about dogma.

'I am terribly short-sighted. Might I come closer?' said Mimi, coming further into the room.

Fitzroy, who had remained concentrating on his work, turned round slowly. 'I would be delighted to show you,' he said. 'I am not as proficient as some in this work, but I have used it effectively before.'

Mimi took a couple of steps further towards him. She turned her head from side to side like a bird hunting a worm. Fitzroy deftly flipped over his drawing. 'If you come and look through this lens,' he said, 'you will be able to make out the ridges and valleys of this person's fingerprint quite clearly. It is one of my strongest lenses.' He stepped aside to let her see.

Mimi came in close and peered at the spectacle. I noticed she kept her hands clasped behind her back. I noticed too that they were empty and then upbraided myself for being foolish. Mimi was far too frail to be a killer.

'Goodness, I can indeed see a mark,' she said. 'I presume it is yours as that boy broke all the glasses.' She straightened up to look Fitzroy in the face. She could not see eye to eye with him, but she was a lot taller than I had thought. I realised she must have been deliberately walking with a hunch. Perhaps she had wanted to seem older and frailer than she was. I could feel the hair rising along my forearms – a sure sign that something was amiss.

Fitzroy smiled one of his most charming smiles and took another step back. This put a little space between them. 'I'm sure I heard Mrs Stapleford say that it was the trifle and trifle bowls that were broken.'

'Yes, Lady Stapleford is a quick thinker. Very beautiful too. Are you lovers?'

If Fitzroy was unnerved by the question he didn't show it. 'Alas no, the lady is devoted to her husband and of a far higher moral calibre than I am.'

Mimi took a step towards him, closing the gap between him. 'Oh, I am sure a gentleman as charismatic as yourself could win her round. After all, it will have been her looks that first made you select her. I imagine with suitable training she could seduce any man she wanted. And who better to give her that training but yourself?'

Fitzroy's tone became colder. 'This is neither the time nor the place for this type of discussion. The purpose of this gathering was to seek a pathway to peace, and not to gather intelligence on each other.'

Mimi cocked her head to one side. 'Curious, you seem to truly believe that. Von Nacht, such an idiotic name, has been spreading rumours about the two of you since he arrived. Then your little game pretending to be her husband – I presume you killed the girl and this was to put everyone off the scent.'

My shoulders relaxed. For one awful moment I had thought Mimi was the killer, but if she was accusing Fitzroy...

'I presume the dagger is in your possession. Can you transfer fingermarks as well as uncovering them?'

'It is an interesting idea,' said Fitzroy. 'I have never had occasion to try.'

'Before now?' suggested Mimi. 'It would fit with your reputation that you might botch killing the girl. You are known for your reluctance to harm women. I can believe you fled the scene, appalled at what you had done, and charged off into the night. Perhaps even the amnesia was real. Or perhaps it allowed you to play out a fantasy as well as make everyone believe you had nothing to do with the killing?'

'You're most perceptive,' said Fitzroy, 'but in this case you are wrong. I did not kill Esmeralda – did you?'

Mimi laughed at this. The sound was remarkably rich and warm. 'Why would I harm her?'

'I have no idea, but why would I?'

Mimi shrugged. 'A seduction gone wrong?'

'When I set out to seduce someone I do not fail,' said Fitzroy.

Mimi shrugged again and began wandering along the table, examining glasses and lenses, but without touching anything. Those hands remained clasped behind her back.

'So, the dagger remains with that rather unimaginative policeman? You will compare the marks in his presence?'

'I prefer not to comment further.'

She walked up to within a foot of him. 'But I do so want to know,' she said. With lightning speed she picked up a glass and, smashing it against the table, went for Fitzroy with the broken edge. He dodged back, but she nicked the side of his arm. I would have immediately come to his aid were it not for the window imploding behind me.

Chapter Forty-five

Contact with the Enemy

I fell forward as a heavy weight hit me in the small of the back. Glass rained down on me. I took the curtain down as I fell, so that as I automatically rolled to avoid whoever was behind me, I only tangled myself further in the material.

Still, I did not stop moving. It was lucky that I did for I felt the ground struck heavily near where I had been. I heard the sound of a blade slicing into wood. I was blinded by the curtains, which smelled so strongly of death. I had no idea who my assailant was. I could hear the sound of the fight between Mimi and Fitzroy. I heard him give a grunt of pain. It must be bad to make him give away the fact he had been struck.

I rolled again, and above me, like some evil stabbing wasp, the attacker plunged the blade back into the curtain. It was sheer luck that they missed. I needed to get out of this fast, but now there was jagged window glass around me. It couldn't be helped. I rolled myself to one side, then curled into a ball and tried to stand. The weight of the material dragged me down. The blade sliced through again, this time far too close for comfort. I needed to reach the edge of this wretched thing.

This time I did not roll, but fought my way through the material, crawling on my hands and knees. Glass sliced into my right palm, and my hand became slick with blood. Strangely, it didn't hurt. But then trying to avoid a knife-wielding maniac can focus the mind. I managed to pick up a chunk of glass in my left hand.

I pulled my knees underneath me and tried once more to stand.

This time I was not dragged back down. I heard the material, now strained beyond belief, rip and tear. I was standing, but it still clung to my head and shoulders. I didn't stop. I blundered blindly towards the table, all the while attempting to rip what proved to be yards of fabric from my face.

Finally, I was free. I saw Gertrude, dressed in a form-fitting costume, much like the ones I use myself on operations, bearing down upon me, dagger raised, her lips drawn back in a snarl and murder in her eyes. Her movements were quick and lithe. This was no old lady. I had no time for further thought. As she lunged towards me I drew my left hand across her throat.

Time slowed as I saw the red line appear across her skin. She staggered back with her left hand to her throat. She took her hand away to look at the blood and then pressed it hard against her throat once more. The expression on her face was more one of surprise than fear.

I backed away, increasing the distance between us. Vaguely I was aware that the fight in the room had stopped. Then Gertrude made a final lunge towards me. She fell short and went down. She rolled on to her back. The blood was now running freely down her neck and chest, despite the hand she kept pressed to it. Her eyes sought me, and she tried to speak, but all that came from her was a wretched, wet and bloody sound. With what little strength she had left, she drove the dagger once more into the floor, in a final fit of frustration. Then although the blood continued to flow, she stopped moving. Her eyes grew glassy and finally dull.

A howl of pain rent the air. Stunned by the outcome of my action, I turned to see Fitzroy, his shirt covered in streaks of blood, backing away from Mimi. She rushed to her sister's side and fell to her knees. She dropped the glass she had been wielding. She touched Gertrude's face, and then she looked up at me. I have never before or since seen such blazing hatred.

Fitzroy advanced towards her. I was still too shocked to move. Mimi leaped to her feet with a spryness we could not have imagined before. The glass was in her hand again. She held it out in front of her, pointing it first at one of us and then the other. All the time she was backing out of the room. I found my feet and made to flank her. Fitzroy and I closed in on her, but there were still some feet between us. When she reached the door, Mimi turned and fled.

Fitzroy barrelled through the doorway and I followed him, lifting my dress higher than decency allowed. Willoughby, who had relinquished his post by the door, came running towards her from the hallway. She lashed out with her glass as he aimed a punch at her head. She caught his shoulder with the glass, deflecting the blow, so that it smashed into her shoulder. Willoughby clamped his hand to his arm, and blood spurted through his fingers. He fell back. She had been lucky and struck him badly.

She didn't break her stride but ran straight into the hall. Bertram was standing talking to Griffin by the library door. 'She has a knife,' I yelled inaccurately. Mimi held out her shard of glass in front of her again and backed away towards the front door.

'There is nowhere for you to go,' said Fitzroy. 'More people will come. Surrender and you will not be treated harshly.'

Her eyes flickered to him as if she was considering this, but she only increased her pace towards the door. When she got there, she tore the door open and ran out into the night.

'Griffin! Alice! Stay here!' shouted Fitzroy and ran out after her.

My natural impulse was to disobey, but I didn't. Fitzroy rarely spares the time to give me a direct order mid-fight. If he ordered me not to follow he had a good reason. 'Griffin,' I said. 'Willoughby is badly hurt. I'll take you to him.'

Griffin reached into the library and grabbed a medical bag. I should have known Fitzroy would have asked him to be prepared. He ran over to me and I ran towards Willoughby. It was only when he had managed to staunch the flow and save Willoughby's life that I realised my husband was not with us.

'Did you see where Bertram went?'

Griffin gave me a sad look. 'He went after Fitzroy.'

Chapter Forty-six

Justice

It became all confusion. Giles fussed around helping Willoughby to a bedroom. Griffin insisted on looking at the gash in my hand that I had entirely forgotten. 'I will have to sew this up,' he said. 'Come into the library and have a whisky.'

'I have to go after Bertram,' I said.

Griffin took me gently by the arm. 'You don't,' he said. 'Fitzroy has stationed men in the courtyard in the event that someone might attempt to flee. There are more than enough of them to overwhelm one old lady. Besides, they are too far ahead for you to catch now.'

I didn't like this, but I saw the sense of it, so I allowed Griffin to lead me to the library and even to hand me a large whisky. 'I'm not happy giving you anything for the pain,' he said. 'You had already been drinking alcohol at dinner . . . I'm sorry, but this will hurt.'

He sewed my hand up with needle and thread as neatly as any seamstress I have ever known. He kept looking into my face to see how I was coping with the pain. But the truth was after the first shock of the needle piercing my skin, I did not notice it. It might have been the whisky I was drinking, but it was more likely to be that my mind was focused on Bertram. I feared for him. Fitzroy, I was confident, could take care of himself. Although both Mimi and Gertrude had proved to be excellent assassins.

'They weren't old,' I said. 'They were pretending. Russia must have sent us two of its best.'

'But why?' said Griffin. 'And why kill Esmeralda?'

I shook my head. I heard voices in the hallway. Fitzroy shouting for whisky and Bertram calling for people to stand back. My emotions and physical exhaustion crashed in on me. It was over. I slumped in the chair and fell into a deep sleep.

I awoke in my own bed with a cover over me and my husband sitting by my side. I reached out to him. 'You are unharmed?'

'I am well,' said Bertram with a faint smile. 'Griffin says you lost a bit of blood and need to rest, but will be fine in a day or two. Apparently, you have to eat lots!'

'Fitzroy?'

'Storming around downstairs, blaming himself for everything and singing your praises.'

'Mimi?'

'Dead,' said Bertram. 'It's over.'

'But how?'

Bertram grimaced. 'I'd rather not tell you.'

'Well then, I shall have to ask Fitzroy.'

'Who will give it to you in detail,' said Bertram, anger in his voice. He took a deep breath. 'It's better you hear it from me. We don't know if Mimi had an escape plan or if she was panicking. But she ran into the Fens, and not knowing the pathways, she was lost to the waters.'

'You mean she drowned?'

'Yes, quite horribly. I wanted to try and rescue her, but Fitzroy said it was too dangerous. Perhaps it was, but afterwards he said that it was better this way.'

I tried to sit up in bed, but Bertram put a hand on my shoulder. 'Rest,' he said.

'Does this mean you watched her drown?'

Bertram didn't reply but turned his face away from me.

'But why? Why did they do any of this?'

'There is only one possible reason,' said Bertram quietly. 'Russia does not yet want this war to end.'

Epilogue

Von Nacht was the last to leave. I kept mentally reminding myself not to call him Alex. We were not allies. The meeting had not worked, and while Fitzroy might be happy to regard foreign agents as fellow professionals and be amicable, I could not bring myself to do so. I also told myself this was not because I found the man attractive, but I did, and if I hadn't been in love with my husband, I wondered . . . Or perhaps I was looking for some light-hearted flirtation in what had become a very dark time. In war and espionage, your thinking can become so – complicated.

'I am sorry things worked out as they did,' he said. We were alone in the hallway as he waited for the carriage to be brought round.

'I think we all are. It was horrible.'

'I meant, Alice, that we are not to be openly allies. I still mean to argue for peace on the behalf of my masters, but I fear I do not bring enough to the table. I fear for my homeland.'

I could feel myself softening to him once more. 'We all share that fear.'

'I do not like that the Russians turned against us. It makes little sense to me. Surely the Tsar, related to both the British and the German royal families, does not want to see war between them.'

'Perhaps he is wary of taking sides.'

Alex shook his head. I mean von Nacht shook his head. 'There is something else afoot in the world. Something we do not expect,' he said, unconsciously echoing Bertram. He continued, 'I think Fitzroy has an idea of what may be afoot, but he has not shared that with me.'

'Nor with me,' I said honestly.

'You should be wary of him. That he became Bertram when he lost his memory – or lost his mind – is not, I think, a coincidence. He envies your husband. I believe he wishes he fulfilled that role.'

'Von Nacht,' I said sharply.

'No, listen. I say this as one who was almost your ally. I see it in him. I have known him for a long time, and I have never known him to be as obsessed with a woman as he is with you.'

I tried again to protest.

'I know you are an honourable woman, who regards her marriage as sacred.' He gave me a wry smile. 'Or I would have tried harder to win your favour. But Fitzroy lands on his feet. He has always got what he wanted – as if he had some golden charm. If he wants you as his wife – if he ever openly acknowledges that – he will make you his wife and do whatever is necessary to achieve that.'

'You have said more than enough,' I said.

'I mean only to warn you. I wish you well, and I hope that peace will prevail.' He snapped his heels sharply together and gave me a quick bow. He opened the door, and a sharp blast of night air cut me to the quick. The door closed behind him, but the cold lingered in my bones. The carriage pulled up as he descended the steps. If it had not, I think he would have waited outside, and I would not have prevented him from doing so.

Cold, and dismayed by our parting, I headed to the library to find a fire to warm my bones, and a glass of something to warm my spirit. I had my hand on the door handle when I heard voices from within. Very quietly, I opened the door an inch and listened.

'We hope to have children one day,' I heard Bertram say. He sounded in a good mood, amiable and chatty.

'Excellent idea,' said Fitzroy. 'Euphemia will make an extraordinary mother.'

'Would it rule her out of – you know?'

'Spying, you mean? That would be your and her decision. I'd certainly advise against going on field missions while the child was young, and of course while she was expecting.' I could almost hear the blush in his voice.

'But she could do some kind of analysis work? Not just paperwork, but contribute somehow?'

'I should think so. She could even oversee my missions. We all need someone back at home to report to and, well, be reined in by. I imagine she'd have rather more success at that than most.' He laughed.

'Thing is . . .' Here Bertram's voiced became a little muffled as if he had turned away. 'Thing is, I think she would be bored here without your world. She's become . . .'

'She was always a wild one, old chap. I first saw her when I visited her father – what? Five or six years ago now. Didn't speak to her. Didn't even realise who she was at the time. Just a young girl, riding bareback on a horse far too large for her and going hell for leather over the fields. That spirit would have come out one way or another. She's a woman of unusual strength of mind. Someone who faces the unexpected with delight. Please don't tell her I said this, but in many ways she is a far better field operative than I could ever be.'

'Why not tell her?'

'My pride,' he said with a chuckle, 'but also because she lacks experience and can push herself too far. I want her to keep me in the loop of her activities.' His tone had become serious, but he gave another laugh. 'She's not ready to be off the leash!'

'I take it you haven't told her this?'

'I have, but not in those words. I value my existence.'

Both men laughed. 'Another?' asked Bertram. Really, one could almost imagine the two of them were friends. I made a noise over opening the door and went in to join them.

'That is von Nacht gone,' I said.

'And good riddance,' said Bertram, and handed me a glass. 'Come over by the fire,' he went on. 'You must be frozen.' Fitzroy nodded to me and quietly left us alone.

★

Later I found Fitzroy wrapped in a thick coat outside looking up at the moon. He was standing in the middle of the south lawn. The heavy snow had begun to thaw, but this afternoon, as if it was having a last hooray, a light fall had come in once more and painted my garden white. My footsteps crunched through the new layer into the slush beneath as I walked across to him.

'Beautiful, isn't it?' he said without turning round. 'Tried to get Jack to come for a walk, but he wouldn't leave the fireside. Doesn't like getting his paws wet.' He turned to look at me and gave me one of his most charming smiles. 'Do you fancy a stroll? I should tell you I think I have worked a couple of things out.'

I fell into step beside him. 'Such as?'

'I think Colonel Long and Lieutenant Wools were German, not English, soldiers. Bertram overheard Esmeralda talking to them about hiring people. I think she was telling them she was here to try to recruit Hans. Bertram remembered the meaning but not the actual words. Context is king. Like when Esmeralda was talking about the game – she was referring to our game. And I realise, if I had told Morley about all this, I would have been able to check up on them at the start. Mind you, I think they did their best to make it obvious they weren't British.'

'Yes, I can see that now. I think I also worked out who Charlie with his weatherbeaten face was.' I paused. 'You won't like it.'

'Naval Intelligence?' ventured Fitzroy with a sneer.

I nodded. 'But Richenda's letter?'

'There is only one possible conclusion – or at least only one I can suggest,' said Fitzroy.

'You mean Richenda wrote it herself to give her the opportunity to find out what her husband was up to . . .'

'I rather think she discovered more than she wanted to,' said Fitzroy. 'I suspect she meant to surprise him before he thought of any . . . you know what.'

'And Esmeralda was killed?'

'Because her intentions ran counter to those of these particular Russians. From what I've gathered they were not the Tsar's people.'

'So what were Esmeralda's intentions?' I asked.

'I can only give you my most likely surmise. There are parts that remain hidden to me.' He took a deep breath. 'I believe that somewhere during the process of recruiting Hans, she received new orders. I had a good go at translating that German letter you found in her room. It struck me there were several layers of code. It will take me time, attention and sobriety to unscramble it all.'

'Hadn't you—' I began.

Fitzroy caught my hand and squeezed it. 'It doesn't matter,' he said. 'With all the evidence we have I think we can conclude that she was sent to brief – or perhaps persuade – the spies present to consider peace. It may be there are differences of opinions within the German Intelligence Service as to what should happen next, or they might be hedging their bets, I suppose.'

'But how can you know?'

'It's simple,' said Fitzroy, 'I would always send a man to start a fight, and a woman to sue for peace.'

'That's an unusual view for you,' I said, frowning.

'Not really,' said the spymaster. 'Women can be deadly – more deadly than men. But women are always the more compassionate, and the more reasonable. Where a man sees righteous destruction, a woman will see waste of life.'

'I'm not sure I can agree with that,' I said. 'There are circumstances where I would be all for destruction.'

Fitzroy laughed. 'But you, my dear, are unique.'

We walked on, the snow crunching under our feet. I did not want him to ask me what would make me be destructive, so I broke the silence.

'Since we are putting things to rights, will Morley sack us?'

'No, we caught a German agent and killed another. Besides, if you're right about Charlie, he wouldn't want to admit we'd gone rogue.' He laughed suddenly. 'First time Naval Intelligence has done me any good!'

We walked on for a while in what was now a companionable silence. I was fitting all the pieces of the last few days together in my head. We moved further and further from the house. Neither of us was used to being cooped up for so long. We did almost daily physical exercise to stay in the necessary shape for espionage. It was exhilarating to be out of the house. And it seemed we were still to be in our respective careers. I had thought Fitzroy would find a way around dismissal – he had done it many times before – but it was a relief to know how things were going to play out. This reminded me of something else I needed to speak with him about.

'You knew I was listening, didn't you?' He raised an eyebrow; the moonlight sharpened his features and gave him a haughty and even intimidating look. It did not deter me. 'Outside the library. You were talking about keeping me on a leash. You don't even do that with Jack.'

'I'm very familiar with your breathing pattern – and Jack is a most obedient dog.'

'Did you mean what you said – that I could continue to work in the field even if I had children?'

We took the Old Mill Lane without discussion. It rose up to the highest point beside the hay meadow, but the walk was steep and not for the faint of heart. In warmer months I used it as part of my summer training runs. We were unlikely to encounter anyone on it at this time of night. I slipped on the ice but regained my balance.

'I said the decision was yours, but I would advise you not to go on operations while your children are young.' He held out his arm to me. I took it gratefully. The rough road was icier than I had expected, and he was wearing the better boots.

'This is because of your mother, isn't it? The effect her death had on you?'

'I think the loss of a parent for any child, but particularly a young one, has a profoundly detrimental effect. Do you disagree?'

We rounded a bend, and the open bars of a field gate gave a view down across the open fields. Pools of water from the thaw shone like liquid mercury. The stars above were diamond-bright. There was no breeze, and a pervading silence filled the fields except for our low voices and occasionally the mournful cry of a hunting owl. No prey would be above ground tonight. I stood looking out, seeing both the beauty and the hunger beneath.

'No,' I said. 'But an unhappy mother . . .'

Fitzroy squeezed my arm lightly against him. 'I could find more than enough material to keep that brain of yours ticking over, and meetings in London would be easy enough.'

We moved off, this time choosing a cart track through a copse. The branches above us swayed faintly in the breeze, making the moonlight flicker.

'You've thought it all out, haven't you?'

Fitzroy produced a hipflask from under his cloak and took a swig before offering it to me. I took it and sipped. 'That's a smoother brandy than Bertram has ever had,' I said, savouring it. I handed it back to him.

'Seriously? I must give the poor man a bottle or two for Christmas.' He stopped and leaned against an old tree. He let my arm go and turned to face me. There was only a foot or so between us, but all at once it felt like a great gulf, as if he was trying to push away from me. 'Now, Alice, I have always found that the future surprises me. It's foolish to think too far ahead. Right now, we are at war, and it will need all our skill and cunning to serve our country. But what I do know is that whatever happens, you and I have many adventures together yet to come.' He smiled, but there was a sadness in it. I reached out and, taking his hands, I pulled him away from the tree. He didn't resist but looked down at me with a puzzled frown. I turned us towards the way back home, as despite my winter attire I was growing cold. I slipped my arm through his once more, resting my gloved hand lightly on his arm, and leaning ever so slightly into his warmth.

We walked back in silence. Both lost in our own thoughts. Together.

We hope you have enjoyed reading *A Death at Christmas*.

For further information about Caroline Dunford's Euphemia Martins mysteries, and to find out all about Caroline's Hope Stapleford adventures,
visit: caroline-dunford.squarespace.com.

RAISING READERS
Books Build Bright Futures

Dear Reader,

We'd love your attention for one more page to tell you about the crisis in children's reading, and what we can all do.

Studies have shown that reading for fun is the **single biggest predictor of a child's future life chances** – more than family circumstance, parents' educational background or income. It improves academic results, mental health, wealth, communication skills, ambition and happiness.[1]

The number of children reading for fun is in rapid decline. Young people have a lot of competition for their time. In 2024, 1 in 10 children and young people in the UK aged 5 to 18 did not own a single book at home.[2]

Hachette works extensively with schools, libraries and literacy charities, but here are some ways we can all raise more readers:

- Reading to children for just 10 minutes a day makes a difference
- Don't give up if children aren't regular readers – there will be books for them!
- Visit bookshops and libraries to get recommendations
- Encourage them to listen to audiobooks
- Support school libraries
- Give books as gifts

There's a lot more information about how to encourage children to read on our website: **www.RaisingReaders.co.uk**

Thank you for reading.

hachette UK

---

1 OECD, '21st-Century Readers: Developing Literacy Skills in a Digital World', 2021, https://www.oecd.org/en/publications/21st-century-readers_a83d84cb-en.html
2 National Literacy Trust, 'Book Ownership in 2024', November 2024, https://literacytrust.org.uk/research-services/research-reports/book-ownership-in-2024